I0738964

RUNNING HURT

ROCKSTAR LOVE IS COMPLICATED. BUT GUILTY LOVE IS IMPOSSIBLE.

RUNNING HEARTS BOOK ONE

SAFFRON BLU

CONTENTS

BLURB

A concert.
A superstar.
A wayward girl.
What could possibly go wrong?

Saxton, the lead singer of Running Hearts, has one rule.
Don't. Do. Fans.
But a chance meeting with Aimee Jonas smashes the rule to
bits.

Being knocked out by Dominic Saxton wasn't part of Aimee's
game plan.
She falls hard and fast, in more ways than one.

Rockstar love is complicated.
But guilty love is impossible.

And in the end, they might be running hurt.

Running Hurt is the first book in the Running Hearts Series.
Although this is a series each book can be read as a stand
alone.

Please note that Saffron Blu is Australian so there will be Aussie-isms in this book.

This book was tricky to write due to it being set in both Australia and America. It has has been written mainly in US English, but in an effort to keep some of the Australian characters authentic there are Australian words and slang in the chapters that contain their POV.

If you have any questions please don't hesitate to contact Saffron.

Some souls are destined to meet.

CHAPTER ONE

AIMEE

I WALKED through the abandoned corridor feeling more and more lost as I chatted to my best friend on the phone. "Sammy, I'm telling you I'm fucking lost. I can't tell you where I am other than a nondescript abandoned corridor."

"Okay, stop and breathe. We'll figure this out. The band aren't going to be on stage for another twenty minutes, we have plenty of time to find you." Sam let out an excited breath. "Oh, I've got an idea, hang on."

The sound of rustling came through the line, and I pulled the phone away from my ear to glare at it. I glanced around the corridor and decided to keep walking. It had to end somewhere, right?

Voices were getting louder, and relief ran through me knowing someone was nearby. Maybe they'd be able to direct me back to the stands.

Suddenly, something hit me hard, sending a shooting pain down the left side of my body. I dropped to the floor in a pain filled heap.

"Fuck." The word sounded distant as blackness engulfed me.

My eyes flicked open and I saw a blurry face looking down at me. Blinking rapidly, my eyes started to clear and a familiar set of mismatched eyes looked back at me with concern.

"I'm hallucinating…I'm fucked."

That was what it had to be; there was no way Dominic Saxton was crouched beside me on the floor encouraging me back to consciousness. Yes, he may have been in the building but he wasn't going to be walking around and at risk of being hounded by overzealous fans. Wanting to shake this stupid hallucination away I tried to think of what I was doing before it started; *talking to Sam.*

"Sam," I said, pushing to sit up. Moving made my head spin and my stomach churn so I quickly decided lying on the floor was the better option.

A very male chuckle close by had my eyes popping open. Was it still a hallucination if it was just sound?

"I don't go by Sam. And last I checked I wasn't a hallucination." He pulled the same smirk I'd seen a thousand times in his interviews. "I'm Dom," he added.

Dominic Saxton was a singer songwriter whose artist name was just Saxton. His band—Running Hearts—was made up of him, his sister and best friend. Their debut song hit number one worldwide and stayed there for weeks; which was why they were currently doing a sellout world tour.

Sam and I had travelled to America especially to see the concert at the last stop, believing the last was always the best show. We figured it was a great way to get us to travel the world a little, which was something we'd discussed numerous times. I had three kids and, having just come out of a messy divorce, it was good to be able to have some 'me time' while the kids were spending the school holidays with their dad— my douche canoe of an ex-husband.

I'd left Sam in the cafeteria while I followed signs for the bathrooms only to go off track and find myself wandering abandoned corridors.

My hand lifted of its own accord and I poked a finger at his chest, before snatching my hand back. "Huh… you *do* feel real."

Jesus! The knock to my head must've done more damage than I thought. I wished it *were* all a hallucination now.

I tried to sit up again, moving slower than before but Dom pressed his palms against my shoulders effectively holding me to the floor.

"You have some wicked bruises, it's probably best if you don't move. Not until the paramedics check you out anyway." He winced as he looked at my face and I hoped to hell it was just a bruise he was wincing at and not my natural lock.

I could hear fast footsteps approaching.

"This is all they had in the freezer." The voice was female and I couldn't help but wonder who it might be. Being jealous was pointless. He was a rockstar, he probably had a busload of female groupies following him around and doing anything he wanted.

I watched Dom smile at the new arrival and take something off her. "Thanks, Sis."

My jealousy was washed away with that one word.

Sis.

That was right, the band was made up of family—his sister playing the drums alongside him. The media had made a big deal about their brother also being with them for the tour, but he was yet to actually be seen on stage so I had no idea what he'd been doing—and the media didn't seem to know either.

Dom turned his attention back to me. "I've got some ice here that I'm going to press to your cheek. I'll be gentle, I promise."

He didn't wait for me to reply, just reached out and placed

the cold hard pack against the side of my face. I hissed but he didn't relent.

"Matt has gone to get your friend, Sam," Dom explained. "She was still on the cell when you blacked out."

The thought that he might have been trying to distract me from the pain ran through my mind before his sister spoke up. "She was crying bloody murder down the line until one of us told her what was happening."

Dom's eyes were on his sister and I grabbed his arm to get his attention. When his eyes locked on mine I gave him a demanding stare. "She knows I'm okay though, right?"

He swallowed nervously. "Well, you were still out of it when Matt left to find her."

Letting go of his arm I reached around the floor feeling for my phone. Sam was a born worrier which meant she'd be freaking the hell out. "My phone? We need to call her."

His warm hand engulfed my searching one, instantly stilling it. "Matt took it. It'll probably be easier finding her if they keep talking."

I sighed and relaxed on the floor, knowing the only person who could distract her from freaking would have been Matthew Dalcin, Dom's best mate and guitarist. Maybe I should've thanked my lucky stars that it was those three that had knocked me out with the door and not just a random stranger. "Who knocked me out with the door?" I asked. The small frown I attempted caused my face to throb.

Dom weighed me up before grinning. "That depends…are you thinking of suing? Because if so, it was Matt."

I laughed. "Well, since you're a shit liar, I guess it's a good job I'm not the suing type."

He let out his own hearty laugh before fresh voices approached.

"Holy fuck! Aimee, are you alright?" Sam's calm tone

relaxed me in an instant. There may have been worry behind her words, but not a complete freak out so that was good.

"I'm okay as long as I don't move."

Sam crouched down beside me, making Dom move away and stand beside his sister.

"Jesus, Aims, your face is a mess." Sam glared at Dom, and I took a moment to close my eyes. As adrenaline began to leave my body, pain seemed to take over.

"Aims?" Sam's worried tone whispered beside me.

"I feel like I've been hit by a truck." I breathed as shallowly as I could, trying not to move.

More voices caught my attention but I didn't open my eyes. If I did, tears would've fallen and I didn't want to look like a wimp in front of my celebrity crush.

"She's just up here," a new male voice announced.

Two paramedics crouched down beside me, gently pressing at my face. After a few minutes of assessing the rest of my body, the older of the two got up and stepped away.

"Aimee, do you think you'd be able to get up and make it to the stretcher?" the younger paramedic asked.

Taking a moment to assess my body and its relevant aches and pains, I decided the only way I would really know was to try. "I guess I could try."

Very slowly, I moved to an upright position. It hurt, but I could handle it.

The younger paramedic took my left arm and Dom appeared at my right, a hand under my elbow ready to catch me if I fell. I stopped holding my breath once I was laid back on the stretcher and gave Dom a grateful smile for his helping hand. "Thanks."

"Don't thank me. I'm the idiot who opened the door into your face. I'm so sorry about that by the way." He shook his head, wincing again as he looked at my face.

"Do I look that bad?"

"You look awful, Aims," Sam said, stopping at my other side on the stretcher.

"Who is coming with us? There's only room for one," the older paramedic asked.

"That'll be me," Sam stated.

"You will not. If I have to miss the concert, you better take a million photos and record all my favorite songs." The panic was audible in my voice. We had paid so much to be there and there was no way I was letting Sam miss it.

No fucking way!

Sam looked at me, indecision clear on her face.

"I'll go with her," offered the guy who'd brought the paramedics in. He stared at Dom. "I know you'll want to be kept in the loop since you'll be paying her medical expenses."

"I…no, I can pay them myself!" I protested. I'd already told them I wasn't the suing type. I didn't expect him to pay my bills just because he'd opened a door that I happened to be on the other side of.

Dom brushed a strand of hair off my face. The gesture seemed too intimate for someone who'd only just met me but, nevertheless, I liked it. "I caused this. At least let me pay to fix it."

The pleading look he had plastered over his face had me nodding before I'd even thought about it.

"Great. So it's sorted. Sam's going to record your favorite songs for you and my brother, Alberto, is going to accompany you to the hospital. He'll give them my details so they can send me the bill." He looked at his brother, who nodded, and then turned his attention to Sam.

She huffed, but I could see the defeat in her slouched shoulders. She was going to fold. "Fine." Her stern look left Dom and softened as her eyes fell on me. "So, that means you want every song recorded since they're all your favorites."

"Yep, but you love me too much not to do it."

She rolled her eyes. "Ugh, you're right." Turning to Alberto she placed my phone in his hand. "It's Aimee's cell, I'm Sam. You text me the minute the doctors tell you anything." Her tone was insistent and although she hadn't added a threat, I knew one was hiding there somewhere.

He dipped his head. "Sure thing."

The paramedics started to wheel me down the corridor and Alberto kept pace along side us. "She's quite scary, your friend."

The genuine unsettled tone in his voice made me laugh. "Yeah, she can be sometimes."

It didn't take them long to get us loaded into the ambulance and on our way to the hospital. Alberto chatted away to me about all kinds of mundane crap. I think he was just trying to distract me from the pain but the paramedics had given me a green whistle to suck on, which was fabulous. After about five minutes I started to feel lightheaded. I assumed it was the drugs so when the machine beside me started beeping chaotically and the older paramedic's voice started to sound anxious I didn't worry—or maybe that was the drugs too.

I didn't really care, I'd just met my celebrity crush and I was on cloud nine because of it.

CHAPTER TWO

DOM

I WATCHED as they wheeled the pretty blonde away—well, I imagined she was pretty under all that swelling and fresh bruising. I was itching to follow her but I couldn't. I was the star of the show after all, even with the band behind me.

"She'll be fine," Matt said. I turned to reply but quickly realized he wasn't talking to me. He had a comforting hand on her friend Sam's shoulder.

She turned, giving me a glare. "You better hope so."

And I did.

I couldn't understand or explain why I felt so attached to a stranger that I'd met by freak accident, but I was. And watching her fiercely protective friend, I knew I needed to get on her good side if I wanted to see Aimee again.

An idea formed in my head and I gave her an apologetic smile. "I'm sorry. She's in good hands and Al has his orders keep you informed on what's happening, so how about we focus on getting Aimee the best video angle we can?"

Sam sighed. "I'm listening."

Matt smirked and I knew instantly that he was attracted to her. Fiery women were his thing. Some people go for blondes or brunettes, but not Matt. He went for women who were sassy and demanding; women who weren't afraid to give you a piece of her mind when she thought you deserved it.

I grinned. "Well, how does stage side sound?" She frowned, clearly considering it. "And we'll get Aimee a copy of the recording that the studio is doing so you can just enjoy the concert for yourself," I added, knowing that was what I'd planned to do from the moment Aimee had mentioned recording it. Cellphone recorders could never pick up sound as well as the professional setup the studio used which was connected to the microphones and speaker system.

"Fine, but that doesn't mean I forgive you for being a douche and opening that door on her."

I let out an unhappy laugh. "I don't even forgive myself for that so I wouldn't expect you or Aimee to."

Sam glanced down at the cellphone in her hand, worry etched into the frown between her brows.

"Al will call as soon as they tell him anything," Matt reassured her.

"What if they don't tell him anything because he isn't family? We're visiting from Australia, she doesn't even *have* family here." Her voice wobbled and Matt pulled her into his embrace.

"I promise Al will get the info. He's smart, he'll come up with something," I offered hoping to ease her mind. Wanting to make sure he did think of that before telling them he's essentially a stranger, I dropped him a quick text message.

Me: Al, make sure you tell them you're family, I don't care what you have to tell them. You need them to keep you updated on everything.

He replied instantly.

Al: Already done. I'm filling in the paperwork now. She…they've taken her through and will let me see her soon.

Happy that my brother seemed to be on the ball, I shoved my cell back in my pocket.

Kat's cell pinged and I glanced in her direction. "Show time." She clapped her hands together. "Janice is having a fit because we aren't backstage," she said referring to our over-reacting tour manager.

Main acts were always late to get started because it was more suspenseful for the audience. They screamed so much louder when they've waited that couple of extra minutes.

Heading backstage, I veered off towards the changing area knowing I needed to get my first outfit on. The support act was still playing and I could tell I had plenty of time because I recognized it as their second to last song but still, I wanted to be ready before Janice had an aneurism.

I let my mind wander in the direction of Aimee and how she might have been doing at the hospital as I stripped out of my clothes behind the screening that they'd put up for our modesty. It wasn't very private back stage but the screen helped enough. It wasn't like we had dancers or extra back-up singers. The only woman allowed back here, apart from Janice—who made it perfectly clear from the beginning that she was more interested in Kat than she was any of the guys—was Kat and she was my sister. Even the hair and make up team were guys.

Stepping out, dressed and as ready as I ever was, I spotted Matt showing Sam around. I watched as he pulled a chair over to the side of the stage, out of view from the audience but giving her a great view of where we'd be on stage. I grinned when I realized he'd set her up on his side of the stage. He'd always been a massive flirt but he usually made the chicks work for it.

Looked like this one was getting some special treatment.

Like clockwork, Janice stepped out of the shadows three minutes before the support act finished their last song. "Are you ready?"

I nodded, giving her a mock salute because I knew that shit pissed her off and she was a cranky bitch ninety-nine percent of the time…which was probably due to the fact that Kat made it clear she wasn't reciprocating her feelings every time she had the chance.

"I always am, Jan."

She grunted at the shortening of her name. She felt it somehow made our relationship less professional. So, of course, I made sure I did it on a daily basis. "Is everyone else ready?" she asked as her eyes roamed around the backstage area. The second her eyes fell on Sam her brow furrowed.

"Who is she and where the hell is her back stage pass?" she demanded in a tone that carried enough for Matt and Sam to hear.

"She's with Matt and he's her backstage pass." The words had barely left my mouth before she marched off to no doubt give Matt a piece of her mind. She hated not being made aware of the things that were happening back here. It was understandable really, her job as tour manager was to ensure each and every concert ran smoothly. Having strangers stage side could cause all kinds of problems.

Mikey, the lead singer in the support act, came charging off stage. A wide smile spread across his face. "The atmosphere out there tonight is fucking amazing!" The rest of the band joined him, some patting me on the shoulder as they walked past.

I grinned back, their excited energy seeming contagious. "It always is at the last show."

Within seconds the crowd started to chant my name. "*Saxton…Saxton…Saxton…*"

"Sounds like you're wanted." He looked at me, awe in his eyes, and I knew he wanted what I had.

Thousands of screaming fans chanting his name.

The fame that came with being lead singer of the newest, biggest band to hit the charts. But he didn't see the loneliness that it all brought. I'd trade it all in for just one woman to see me for me.

The *real* me.

Not Saxton. Just Dom.

Kat's drumsticks tapping on my shoulder pulled me out of my thoughts. "Jesus, Kat, I wish you wouldn't do that. The bruises will never fade."

Kat threw her head back in a laugh. "I always knew you were a wimp, little bro." She gave me a grin before carrying on. "Besides it's my good luck thing. You kiss your Saint Luke pendant before walking out on stage, I have to tap your shoulders."

I shook my head, knowing it wasn't worth explaining the significance of my good luck 'thing'. Mom gave me the Saint Luke because he supported artists and the one night I didn't kiss it, we had the worst night. Speakers cut out. The whole venue blacked out. I wasn't risking that again. "After 102 shows it's getting pretty old. If we ever tour again you better find a new good luck thing."

"If?" She looked at me wide eyed, like she'd never considered us not touring again. "This is just the beginning of our career, of course we'll be touring again."

"Ready?" Matt asked stepping up beside us.

Pulling out the pendant and pressing my lips to it before dropping it back under my shirt, I turned my attention to him. "I am now."

He held out his fist in a fist bump—his good luck thing—and the three of us connect our fists. "Let's do this!"

Walking to the little cubby under the stage, listening to the excited chatter running through the crowd, was always pretty eerie. It was one of the things I'd miss if we didn't tour again. It wasn't like I planned on giving it all up, but you never knew how long you'd stay on top. There was always the thought, that you could be a one-hit wonder, floating around in the back of your mind. Our next album could be the biggest flop and we could get dropped in a nanosecond.

Taking one last calming breath, I stepped onto the platform and turned to the microphone stand.

The crowd got louder as the guys moved into their positions on stage, probably only able to see their dark silhouettes.

Kat beat out a rhythm on her drum kit.

The crowd cheered and clapped along to the beat.

The stage hand crouched in front of my platform gave me a thumbs up and only when I returned the gesture did the platform begin to rise.

Dom disappeared and Saxton came to life.

CHAPTER THREE

DOM

WE WERE DIRECTED into a private waiting room the minute we arrived at the hospital. I had a cap pulled down low, hiding the majority of my face, but I still heard the whispers of my name. Not being able to go about your day without being recognized was a pain in the ass, especially in times like this.

Once the doors were closed on us, I stepped forward to descend on my brother, only to find him backing away from an angry brunette and into the blind-covered windows.

"What the fuck did you not understand about text me the minute the doctors told you anything?" She shoved at his chest. He remained silent but flicked his eyes to mine over her shoulder. "Don't look to him for help. Speak!" Sam took a step back, giving him some space.

Al sighed and rubbed a hand over his face, before dropping into the nearest seat and focusing on Sam. "The doctors made it clear they were doing everything they could and you rushing here, missing the concert..." He locked his eyes on mine. "Cancelling the concert..." He grimaced. "It wouldn't have done anything to help Aimee. It would have just given you more time to freak out and worry. I'm sorry, but I thought it was what Aimee would want. She wanted you to stay at the concert, that's why I'm even here in the first place."

Sam let out a furious grunt. "Don't you dare pretend you know what Aimee would want."

She stormed towards the red door but before she got close enough to reach the handle it opened and a middle-aged guy in a white coat stepped into the room, closing the door behind him.

"I've been told you're Aimee's family," he started.

I removed the ball-cap and threw it on the little coffee table in the middle of the room.

"Mr. Saxton, I'm Doctor Kris Petrov." He offered his hand as he carried on. "I've been treating your wife."

My eyes almost popped out of my head at his words. I'd known Al would come up with something to get the information, but *my* wife? Why the hell didn't *he* just play husband?

Obviously seeing my shock the doctor flicked his eyes around the room taking in everyone's look of surprise. "She *is* your wife, right? Because unless you are immediate family, I can't tell you anything."

Sam smiled and offered out her hand to the doctor. "Hi, I'm Sam, Aimee's life long best friend, I was maid of honor. I know for a fact they are husband and wife." She grabbed my hand as if she'd done it a million times. "Mr. Saxton here was just a little surprised because it's a secret for the time being. The newly weds have been able to enjoy the privacy that his fame doesn't always allow."

"Of course." The doctor gave us a warm smile like he understood, an understanding I wished I had. I could see this completely blowing up in our faces. I was desperate to question my brother about where his head had been at, but first we needed to hear about Aimee and then get rid of the doctor.

"So…my wife? How is she?" I asked.

The doctor's features softened and I didn't like it one bit. It felt like he had sympathy for me and if that was the case, it would mean whatever he had to tell us wasn't good news. I held Sam's hand tightly in mine, hoping to give her some comfort—After all, Aimee was her friend.

"Due to the brain trauma Aimee suffered we had to put her into a medically induced coma. Now, I know that sounds scary, but it isn't as bad as it sounds. It's the best thing for her in this case. We're just giving her body the time it needs to heal." The doctor's eyes were full of sympathy behind his glasses.

I nodded.

Sam spoke up. "When will she wake up?"

Dr. Petrov pushed his glasses up the bridge of his nose. "Well, that's something we don't know. Everyone is different. Best case…a couple of days…"

Sam's hand squeezed mine briefly and I knew what she wanted to ask. So I did it for her. "And the worst case?"

He sighed as if he hoped we wouldn't ask. "A few weeks."

Sam gasped beside me before she dropped my hand and started to pace the small waiting area. "Aimee is strong. She'll be okay." It was like she was reminding herself of that rather than actually meaning to say it to anyone. "When can we see her?" she asked.

Dr. Petrov allowed his eyes to roam around the room, taking in the five of us. "As soon as we have her in a private room I'll send a nurse up to get you. You'll only be able to see her two at a time, though."

"Okay. Thank you," I stated. Taking it as a dismissal, he rushed out of the room as though he couldn't escape quickly enough.

I rounded on Alberto. "What the *fuck* were you thinking?"

He stayed seated, shoulders slumped in defeat, and the sight of him like that took some of the fight out of me. "I wasn't. The paramedics assumed you were her boyfriend and I just ran with that. When I filled out the paperwork, I ticked husband thinking boyfriend probably wouldn't be enough to get the information."

I sat opposite him and rubbed a hand over my face, as exhaustion crept in. "You do realize there's going to be a shit storm once the press gets a hold of this?"

Kat dropped down beside me. "It might not even get out. The hospital isn't going say anything, they don't want the corridors full of paparazzi."

"I'm not worried about the press turning up here. I'm more worried about word of my *secret marriage* getting out," I admitted.

"There is no fucking marriage. It'll be nothing more than a rumor." Sam's angry voice called across the room. "Aimee's up there, strapped to god only knows how many machines and all you care about is the press getting information on you that could harm your career. You're the reason she's up there and if I didn't need you to get information from the doctors, I'd have kicked you out by now."

"I couldn't give a damn about my career. I'm more bothered about them harassing Aimee when she wakes up and tries to get back to her life."

At my admission, Sam stared at me, her eyes wide in surprise, and I realized she really had thought I was all about myself, and my career — and didn't that just grate on me.

CHAPTER FOUR

AIMEE

GENTLE FINGERS PRESSED against the pulse point on my wrist and I fought to open my heavy eyelids. I caught sight of a woman who was looking at her watch, her lips moving slightly as she obviously counted the beats. I must have made some noise because her eyes flicked to mine and a big smile crossed her face.

"You're awake. Your family is going to be so happy."

I frowned at her words. Awake? Why wouldn't I be awake? I opened my mouth to speak but my throat was so dry all I could do was choke.

"Here." She held out a glass of water, guiding a straw between my lips. "Slowly," she warned as I pulled at the cool liquid.

"Your husband hasn't left your side. He'll be so glad to see you awake," she said, keeping her tone hushed.

Once again, I frowned. Husband? I didn't have a husband…did I?

She bobbed her head towards a small foldout bed where a dark-haired male was curled up, clearly sleeping, in front of the window. The curtains were drawn and the room was dark, the only light coming in from the open doorway, so I couldn't make much out.

The sound of a snoring man rolled through my mind. A memory. *My ex-husband.* He'd been a snorer. The guy on the foldout bed wasn't snoring. So I knew that wasn't him. Did I have another husband I didn't remember?

I could tell from the nurse and the beeping equipment that I was in a hospital, but I didn't remember how I'd gotten there. Turning my attention from the sleeping guy back to the nurse, I asked her one of the many questions floating through my mind. "How long?" She frowned. "You said he hadn't left my side. How long has that been?"

She made an 'O' of her mouth, before picking my chart up off the end of the bed. "Let's see… You were admitted five days ago."

"Five days? I don't remember…" Panic flowed through me. How could I have been here five days and not remember any of it? My heart started to race and the machine began to beep louder. My breath was becoming erratic and I worried I'd pass out if I didn't calm down.

"I'll get the doctor," I heard the nurse announce.

A warm hand slipped into mine and I glanced down at it to see a male hand, his thumb rubbing over my wrist.

"Aimee. It's okay. I've got you. Breathe."

I lifted my head and found myself face to face with Dominic Saxton. The concern in his mismatched eyes sent me back to a bleak corridor where he'd stared down at me with that exact same look.

"Dom…" His name fell off my lips.

He beamed at me. "At least you don't think I'm an hallucination this time." He tucked a strand of my hair behind my ear like it was second nature to him.

My face heated at the intimacy of his touch.

"So, five days?" I blinked as my mind did some really slow

calculations. The concert had been two days before our flight home. "Where's Sam?" I asked, knowing the answer before he even gave it.

Letting go of my hand, he grabbed a chair and pulled it up to the bed before taking my hand in his once again. "She had to go home. I offered to pay for a new flight so she could stay but they wouldn't extend her visa because she wasn't family. I even tried to sponsor her for however long it took until you could fly, but they wouldn't allow it." He grimaced. "She was so pissed; I'll be surprised to hear Matt didn't have to drag her on the plane kicking and screaming."

My eyes widened in shock. "Matt? Matt went with her?"

Dom scratched at the back of his neck, clearly embarrassed about something.

"Mrs. Saxton. How are you feeling? Nurse Sharon said you were a little panicked when you woke up." I turned my attention to the doctor striding towards the bed, schooling my features into a straight face. The nurse had referred to Dom as my husband and I was alert enough to understand I should play along rather than question it.

"I was a little panicked, not knowing where I was or how I got here, but once my husband held my hand I knew I was safe." I gave Dom a doe-eyed expression hoping to prove our fake relationship to the doctor. It wasn't exactly hard. Dominic Saxton could probably get any number of girls giving him doe-eyes.

Dom frowned but played along, lifting my hand and pressing a kiss to the back of it.

"Do you mind if I quickly check you over?" the doc asked.

I shook my head and he got down to business, pressing buttons on the machine beside me until a cuff around my arm started to tighten. He then made me look in different directions while following his finger before he shone a flashlight in both my eyes. Whatever he was seeing he must have been happy with because he said as much. "Good." He glanced at his watch. "It's late, so first thing tomorrow we'll get you started with some physiotherapy. We want to get you moving as soon as possible." He quickly bid us both good night before disappearing out the door.

Nurse Sharon quickly poked her head in the door. "He just did all your obs didn't he?" Dom and I both nodded. "I'll be back in a few hours then. If you need anything just push the buzzer." She pointed to behind the bed and I figured I'd find it if I needed anything.

"So…?"

He grinned. "So…?" he repeated my words.

I laughed. "I've got so many questions, I'm not sure which one to start with."

He settled back in his chair as though he was getting comfy. "Well, I'm not going anywhere, so…hit me with them all."

I tried to push myself up into a sitting position and failed miserably.

Dom jumped up and with a quick hand under each of my arms he had me lifted into a comfortable upright position. "Better?" he asked hovering over me, ready to fix it if I said no.

"Yes. Thank you." I frowned as I watched him sit back down. "Why…why are you here?"

He gave me a look I couldn't quite put my finger on. "I'm the one that put you here. It's all my fault." His words made me realize it was guilt I'd seen on his face.

My heart sank. I didn't want him to be here out of guilt when he had no reason to feel it. "It was a freak accident. You didn't do it intentionally. And anyway, I remember you saying you were paying my medical bills, so surely that makes us square now. Yet, you're still here." My lips felt dry and I licked them to try moistening them.

Grabbing my glass off the side table he offered it to me straw first. I took a sip and smiled gratefully when I was done. Placing the glass back down, he stood and walked over to the window, peaking out the side of the blinds. I could tell he wanted to see the night outside and, to be honest, so did I.

"Could you open those? I'd love to see what's out there."

Dom pulled the cords and the blinds opened revealing a clear night sky. There were plenty of stars to be seen, and I could imagine how beautiful it would look away from the bright lights of the city.

"Do you want me to be honest?" Dom asked, breaking the silence.

I frowned at his question. "Of course. That's all I ever want off anyone."

Dom nodded. "I'll remember that." He sighed and with one last look at the night outside he strode back over to his chair and took a seat once again. "I don't know why I'm still here. Other than the fact that deep down, I feel like I need to be." He laughed, an almost sad sound. "Have you ever met someone and felt that you were meant to meet?"

I was suddenly concerned about him. Had he hit his head at some point too? "Dom," I started, unsure of what else to say.

"I know I sound crazy, just pretend I didn't say that. I'm a creative person and it makes me say and do the weirdest crap."

I laughed. Being a writer, I've used that excuse many times myself. "I'm a writer. I *get* creative crazy."

"Ah, yes. Sam said you both were writers."

It was weird thinking he knew things about me that hadn't come from me. I knew Sam would never share anything I wouldn't want sharing but I found myself suddenly wondering what she might have told him.

Did he know I have kids?

Did he know I'm divorced?

I mentally kicked myself for thinking such stupid shit. It wasn't like those things would matter. He wouldn't be interested in someone like me anyway.

Dom was only there because he felt responsible.

"Sam… It sounds like you guys got to know each other." I'd be lying if I didn't admit the thought made me a little jealous. "And you didn't answer my question earlier… Matt went home with her?"

"Not really. Sam blames me for what happened to you so there was no chance of us becoming best friends." He smirked. "Matt on the other hand… Well, they hit it off. Since the tour was finished he had time to spare so he decided to go and see some of Australia… and give Sam some company on the flight over."

"Is my phone handy?" I tried to look at the table but just couldn't see it from the angle I sat at. "I guess I should probably call my family."

Dom lifted his arm to look at his watch. "Shit. I should have called your mom by now."

My eyes almost popped out my head at his admission. "You've been calling my mum?"

He tapped at—what I recognized as—my phone a few times. "We've actually been Face Timing. Here…"

The sound of a call going through came out of my phone speakers and within seconds my mum's voice followed. The sound filling me with a familiar comfort. "Dom, you're late."

"I know, Sarah." Hearing him speak to my mum on a personal level, calling her by her first name, was strange to me. "I'm sorry but I do have a good reason for it. Here…"

Dom turned the screen so it faced me and I could see my mum's surprised face on the screen.

"You're awake?" She burst into tears. "She's awake. Aimee's awake," she called out to whoever was with her. Her voice was full of emotion and I wished I were there to give her a hug.

"Maybe I should have broken the news another way." Dom glanced at me, concern clear in his wide eyes.

Mum wiped at her eyes. "Happy tears. They're happy tears, Dom."

It was heartening to see Dom's concern towards my family. I patted the bed beside me in invitation and Dom slid into the space without a word. We both watched Mum wiping at her tears.

"Boys, come here, your mum's awake," she called out before glancing back at the screen. "You two look cute together."

"*Mum!*" I admonished, embarrassment making my cheeks heat.

She waved her hand dismissively. "Pfft…you haven't had a date in forever. A mother can hope."

I hid my face behind my hands; suddenly wishing a hole would swallow me up. I couldn't believe she'd say such thing.

Dom laughed and I slapped at his bicep, making the phone shake. "Don't encourage her."

My youngest son's face filled up the screen.

"Dan…" I was lost for words. I should be home with them not in a hospital bed half a world away.

"Mummy. You're okay? Dom had said you'd be okay, but…" I was surprised to here Dan speak about Dom like they knew each other. It meant he'd gone above and beyond to make my family feel like I was in safe hands. I filed that fact away for later so I could thank him for it.

"I'm okay." I nodded and smiled, grateful that the bad

lighting didn't show the bruises I knew where there. I'd been laid in a bed for five days after having a fight with a door. I was pretty sure I looked awful.

One of my older sons pushed his way in front of the screen. "Mum, when are you coming home?"

"Reece, I'm not sure. The doctor said he wants to get me moving around tomorrow so hopefully that's a good sign. I'll ask him tomorrow."

He grinned at me. "Good, because we miss you."

A whole heap of voices echoed his words and I wiped a tear from the corner of my eye. "I miss you guys too."

"Okay… We're gonna let you get some rest. Dom, call me again tomorrow when the doctor's seen her," my mum ordered.

"I am here." I stated, but they both ignored me.

Dom instead talked over the top of me. "Will do, Boss."

I shook my head as Dom cut the call and dropped the phone into his lap. He didn't move away like I'd expected, which surprisingly made me happy. It was nice feeling his warmth against my side. It comforted me in a way, making me feel like I wasn't in this alone.

I still didn't understand why he was here for me? Why he hadn't just paid the bills and gone home?

But whatever the reason, it was nice having someone by my side in this quiet room.

CHAPTER FIVE

DOM

THE NEXT FEW days passed with tests after more tests followed by physiotherapy sessions after more physiotherapy sessions. Aimee wanted to get home to her family as soon as possible so she was pushing herself hard. I could see that she was in pain, but not once did it stop her from hitting that next target. Be it a longer stretch or a heavier weight.

On the fifth morning after Aimee woke from her coma, Dr. Petrov entered the room with a wide smile on his face. "Good morning."

Both Aimee and I smiled but didn't speak; I think we were both too eager to hear what had put such a big smile on his face.

"Aimee, you've made some great progress. Your movement seems to be what it should have been before the incident, and looking at your latest scan results shows you are most definitely out of danger."

Aimee sat up straighter on the bed. "Does that mean I can go home?"

My heart sunk at her words.

I knew she'd have to go home eventually but I enjoyed

our chats late into the night and the silly board games we'd been playing to keep ourselves entertained — board games I'd had to beg, borrow or steal from the pediatric ward.

It wasn't like Aimee going home would mean I was going to be walking out of her life. No, in fact long before she woke up I'd already made plans to fly home with her and spend some time in Australia. My best friend, Matt, was there and we hadn't had much chance to see any of it when we'd flown in to do our one night concert there a few months back.

Not that I'd been brave enough to tell her that yet. *What if she didn't want me to go?*

I was going to miss having her to myself.

"Not just yet," Dr. Petrov started. "I am going to discharge you from the hospital but I want to see you back here in a week for one more check up, and then I'll see about giving you the green light to fly home." He scribbled on Aimee's chart, before ripping off a sheet of paper and placing it on the tray table at the end of the bed. "Here are your papers. Mr. Saxton, your insurance company will want a copy. Aimee, when I see you next week I'll give you some more papers for you to pass on to your doctors back home."

"Okay," Aimee said, sounding uncertain. I glanced at her to see if I could work out what she was thinking but whatever it was I couldn't read in her features.

"Just make sure you leave a contact number on your way out and we'll call to arrange a time for your check up." Tucking Aimee's chart under his arm Dr. Petrov walked out of the room throwing a quick "goodbye" over his shoulder.

Aimee grabbed her cell off the table and started furiously clicking at the screen like she was on a mission.

Placing my hands over hers, I stilled her fingers, pushing the cell to the bed. "What's bothering you? I thought you'd be excited at the prospect of going home."

She let out a big sigh, a sure sign she wasn't happy

about something. "I just thought I'd be able to go straight home when they release me. Now I've got to find a hotel to stay at for the next week and bide my time there until I get the green light to fly. I'm just frustrated I have to wait longer."

Realizing I could make things a little easier for her, I took her cell out of her hands. "Give me that. Go get showered," I screwed up my face in mock disgust, "because you stink."

She slapped at my arm. "I smell just as bad as you do," she said causing me to laugh, because it was the truth, I'd showered just as much as she had the last few days.

"I'll have our accommodation figured out by the time you're ready to go."

My eyes widened in surprise as she planted a peck on my cheek. "Thank you." Grabbing the bag she'd been living out of, she shut herself in the bathroom and I made a few calls, all the while my heart pattered away as I felt the remnants of her kiss on my cheek.

———

FIFTEEN MINUTES LATER, Aimee was standing by the bed brushing her long blonde hair and ordering me to get showered. I did so without argument, because she'd been right, I was feeling a little ripe, and we'd need a four and a half hour car journey to get to our accommodation.

I was taking her home.

To the house I grew up in.

Home to my family.

My mom had been ecstatic when I'd asked if she'd be okay with having a guest at such short notice. I never really dated, and I'd never brought a girl home, so understandably my mom was already planning the wedding.

I chuckled to myself, thinking about it as I dried myself

off. Mom had always been trying to marry us kids off. I personally thought it was the grandkids she wanted the most.

I walked out the bathroom to find Aimee sat on the bed, flicking through her cell. She lifted her eyes, slowly trailing them up my body before licking her lips as they locked on mine.

"Sorry, I forgot my clothes," I admitted as I held my hand in front of my towel-covered dick, trying to hide my growing erection caused by the way her eyes all but ate me up.

Aimee cleared her throat, a pink blush covering her face. "I'm…just going to give the nurse my number," she muttered as she rushed out the door.

Making quick work of throwing my clothes on, I grabbed both mine, and Aimee's bags off the bed before heading out to find Aimee. I found her chatting to a male nurse that had spent a couple of hours after his shifts watching Netflix shows with us on Aimee's laptop.

"I'm going to miss you, Oz. Make sure you come and say hi before you leave the country, okay?" Josh said as he pressed a kiss to the top of her head. I was envious of how comfortable he was doing such a thing.

A thing I'd wanted to do for days.

She pulled back and gave him eye contact. "Promise."

"Did you pack everything, Aims?" I asked, knowing she would have. Over the last few days we'd spent together I'd gotten to know her pretty well and I could see she was a triple checker when it came to making sure things were done.

Josh dropped his arms from around Aimee and she stepped away. "Yep, I triple-checked all the drawers and made sure to put your phone and charger in the front pocket of your bag too."

I gave her a grateful smile. I hadn't even thought about my cell which had been on charge.

"Catch you later, Dom. You might want to shove on a cap

before you head out," Josh offered, reminding me that I wasn't just a regular Joe.

I'd gotten so comfortable in my own skin over this last ten days with the nurses and doctors treating me like a regular person that I'd forgotten I was an easily recognizable singer who often had press following me around. I glanced down at the bags trying to think where the cap I'd worn all those days ago may have gotten to.

"I think there was one in the front pocket where I put your phone," Aimee stated as she took a step towards me.

Taking her word for it I placed both our bags down and found my cap exactly where Aimee had thought it was. After tugging it on and throwing our bags over my shoulder I turned to her. "You ready?"

She nodded and waved goodbye to Josh before falling in step beside me. My nerves were a complete mess. I had no idea what we'd find waiting for us outside.

Alberto and my dad had both driven down a few days ago and left one of my parents' cars, thinking I'd probably need one at some point, whether it was just to get us to the airport —not that my parents knew I was planning on going too, they probably just assumed I'd be dropping her off and then driving home—or to drive us around for a few days.

I patted my pocket, feeling the bulky car keys inside them.

"So, where are we going?" Aimee asked, breaking the silence between us.

Not wanting her to worry about my family I said the only thing I could think of. "It's a surprise."

We made it to the car without any trouble from the press or fans. I popped the trunk and dropped our bags in side as Aimee let herself into the front of the car, first opening the driver's side before correcting herself and walking around to the passenger side with a laugh.

"I forgot you guys are weird and drive on the wrong side of the road."

I chuckled at her words as I slid behind the wheel. It was a good job I was driving then, otherwise we'd have probably ended up back in the hospital.

My cell started to ring just as I pulled out of the parking space. The ringtone was the one I'd set exclusively for the record label. Aimee gave me a sideways glance but I shrugged it away. "If it's important they'll leave a message."

As we drove down the road I spotted a drive-thru, and knowing we had a long drive ahead of us I made a decision to grab us some food.

"Are you hungry already?" Aimee asked as I pulled off the road.

I rubbed my stomach. "That hospital food made me feel like my throat's been cut." She laughed and I quickly asked what she wanted as we pulled up to the speaker.

I rattled off our order to the loud crackling voice, hoping to hell they get at least something right in the end. I didn't want to have to go inside to get the order fixed and I didn't want to make Aimee do it.

Not when she had a cute Australian accent. They either wouldn't understand her or would want to steal her away from me.

As I pulled to a stop outside the collection window and an excited scream pierced the air.

"*Oh my god!* It's really you!" a girl's wobbly voice called out.

"Jayne, what the hell is going on here?" an older sounding female voice asked, getting closer with each word.

I glanced inside and saw a pretty blonde girl who looked no older than sixteen, giving me a doe-eyed expression.

"It's Saxton. *The* Saxton…At the window," she said,

clearly trying to explain her reaction to the woman wearing a manager's badge.

The older woman bent down to look at me through the open window and I gave her a brief wave and smile. "Holy crap, you're right." After a quick shake of her head she straightened and turned her attention to the staff in her vicinity. "We have customers waiting. Let's be professional here and give the man his food."

I could hear mumbled agreement and the sounds of people dashing about before the young girl leaned out of the window telling me how much I owed.

Aimee having unbuckled her seatbelt stretched over me and put her card in the girl's hand. "I'll pay." Her eyes fell on me as the girl took the payment. "You've done so much for me lately, I think I can at least buy you a burger."

The girl handed back the card and receipt before giving me a sheepish look while holding a pen and napkin out to me. "Is there any chance I could get an autograph?"

Taking note of the name on her badge I wrote a quick personalized note on the napkin, ending it with a squiggle that had become my 'Saxton' signature. People thought it strange that it was nothing like my personal signature even though it was my surname, but I just figured it was safer having different ones. I never minded giving autographs or having selfies with fans but having Aimee beside me made it feel little odd. I'd just been me when I'd been with her at the hospital, not Saxton.

Holding the napkin close to her chest Jayne stepped back as the manager passed me the bag of food out of the window, offering an apology for the reaction and slow service.

Aimee took the bag out of my hands in silence and I drove out of the drive-thru. I'd originally planned to eat in the parking lot but since I'd been recognized it was probably be best to move on to somewhere else. I kept on driving until I spotted a quiet little side street, my stomach grumbling the whole time. I really wasn't kidding when I'd said I was hungry.

Aimee grabbed her items, before blindly shoving the bag in my direction. I laughed as I took it off her hands.

After picking out the pickle she took a big bite, moaning while she chewed. "Oh my god… I think this is the best dirty burger I've ever had."

I washed a bite of burger down with my soda before turning my attention to her. "Dirty burger?" I questioned, feeling the frown form on my face.

She sucked on her straw and I watched her cheeks hollow, which gave me all kinds of naughty thoughts I probably shouldn't be having.

"You know? Greasy and really bad for your health, but it tastes oh-so-good…" She shrugged. "That's a dirty burger."

I threw the empty burger wrapper in the bag and pulled out my pouch of fries. I munched on them as I watched an older couple walk by the car hand in hand. The woman looked up at the man with so much love I practically felt it. It was the kind of love I'd craved for a long time.

When fame hit, I'd thought the music and the love of fans would be enough to keep me happy. Unfortunately, it didn't even come close.

"So, are you ready to tell me about this surprise yet?" Aimee's question pulled me out of my thoughts.

Taking my time, I licked the salt off my fingers while I decided what to tell her… if anything. Just as I opened my mouth my cell rang. The ringtone once again told me it was my record manager and the fact that I'd already ignored his call once made me think I should probably answer it this time. I pulled my cell from my pocket and clicked accept.

"Hey."

"Sax, are you still in New York City?" Gary's voice was strained and it put me on edge.

"I am," I answered. My uncertainty caught Aimee's attention and she glanced my way. I gave her a quick smile hoping to dislodge the concern I could see on her face.

Aimee quietly grabbed the trash and pointed outside the car to a trashcan up the road.

I nodded, while I listened to Gary. "We need to chat. Can you come into the office before you leave the city?"

"Yeah, sure." I didn't particularly want to go but he was my boss, and if he wanted a chat I had no option but to go and listen.

Running Hearts wouldn't be what we are without him.

I owed him my career.

Aimee got back in the car just as I slid my cell back in my pocket.

"I've got to go see my record manager. Do you mind a little detour before we start for where we're headed?"

Aimee shrugged. "It's not like I know our destination anyway," she said with a smile, a smile that I was beginning to love to see.

CHAPTER SIX

AIMEE

WALKING into the record company's swanky office had my palms sweating and my heart racing. I hated going places where I felt I didn't belong, and this posh building was far from where I belonged. I took a deep breath, trying to calm my stupid anxiety.

"You okay?" Dom asked quietly, giving me a wary glance as he held the door open for me.

I tried to give him what I thought was a reassuring smile, but the frown on his face told me I failed.

"Saxton. Thank god. Go straight through," a woman's voice, full of relief, called out.

Dom looked at me uncertainly, probably not wanting to leave me. I gestured towards a sofa against the wall, which I assumed was a waiting area. "I'll just be there, texting the kids."

It wasn't exactly a lie. I'd already texted the kids, they just hadn't replied yet. They were never in a hurry to reply to messages, and they absolutely never initiated contact.

Unless they wanted something from me.

I sure hoped it was something they'd grow out of because

I didn't think I could live with that lack of connection for the rest of my life.

I rubbed a hand over the ache in my chest at missing my kids as I typed out a quick message to my best friend. I'd been in touch with Sam on a daily basis since waking up and, although she never really mentioned what was happening with her currently, I knew she was one person who appreciated my messages. As I slipped my phone into my handbag the chair dipped alerting me to someone sitting beside me. I looked up to find the current hottest rapper to hit the charts, Darius, looking back at me.

"Hey." My face flamed as I realized my voice sounded way too high-pitched. *Be cool, Aimee. Do not act like a fool.*

"Hey. Did it hurt?" Darius asked, a wide grin on his face.

I frowned. "Hurt?" I raised a hand to my face, suddenly conscious of the fading bruises.

"When you fell from heaven."

I groaned.

"You did *not* just say that!" the receptionist called over the counter.

Darius chuckled before turning serious. "But seriously, those bruises… Are you okay?"

I did resemble someone who had gone ten rounds in a boxing ring and not come out the winner, but I'd seriously thought they weren't looking so bad now. Perhaps I was just getting used to them.

Feeling at ease with him I gave him a smile. "I don't look half as bad as I did."

"Should I be hunting someone down?" I frowned at his words. "The person that did that to you."

I shook my head. "No. It…I walked into a door."

He didn't believe me, I could tell by his clenched jaw. "Seriously, whoever did that to you deserves a good beating."

I opened my mouth to explain more when Dom stepped out the office, his eyes falling first on me, and then Darius.

"D." He nods. "You ready, Aims?"

The shortening of my name made butterflies take flight in my stomach, just like it had every time he'd done it in the last few days. There was something intimate about it and I liked it.

I liked it a lot.

Not that I should be stupid enough to get used to it. Once I headed back to Australia, I wouldn't be seeing or hearing from him again.

I gave him a warm smile as I got to my feet.

"Sax…" Darius glanced from Dom to me and back again, a broad smile on his face. "It all makes sense now. Mrs. Saxton, nice to meet you." He gave me a mock bow.

I was glad he thought it made sense because I was completely lost. I frowned. No one had called me that since the first day of me waking from the coma. We came clean with the hospital staff as soon as we knew they'd allow Dom to stay whether we were married or not. Since they'd already let him stay for the time I was comatose they hadn't seen an issue with him staying longer. It wasn't like we were noisy or causing a fuss. In fact, they decided it was better to allow him to stay than having him come in and out during visiting times and causing chaos with the paparazzi.

"You've lost me," I stated as I shook my head in hopes of making something fall into place.

Dom swallowed audibly and I gave him a curious stare. *What the fuck was I missing?* I opened my mouth to ask exactly that when another guy stepped out from the office Dom just exited.

"Nice to meet you, Aimee. You've definitely put a spanner in the works for us."

Dom's hands fisted at his sides. "Gary, drop it."

The receptionist gasped, and I wondered if Dom was going to get in trouble for speaking to whom he'd referred to as his boss like that.

Gary held up his hands in surrender and turned his attention to Darius. "Come on in, D." He spun on his heel and led the way back in to his office Darius following behind.

I watched the door close before I locked eyes with Dom. "You're gonna explain all this to me, aren't you?" I asked, waving my hand in a circle to describe what *this* I was referring to.

Dom sighed, his lips pinched together tightly. "Yep, we've got a four hour drive to Cold Springs after all."

Cold Springs rang a bell and I scratched my cheek as I tried to figure out why.

"You're taking her home?" the receptionist asked, weighing me up over the counter. She hadn't really paid me much attention before and I felt uncomfortable under her scrutiny. "I can't decide if Gary will think that's good news or bad."

Dom huffed and headed out the door, completely ignoring her. "Let's go," he said to me.

I followed silently, wondering what to worry about first. Should it be the fact that Dom didn't deny taking me home or that they all seemed to know something that I didn't? Darius's comment about me being Mrs. Saxton had me concerned about whether the media had gotten hold of something I wasn't aware of.

There was only one way to find out for sure.

As we walked through the parking lot, I pulled out my phone and Googled 'Saxton'. A number of news articles popped up but the one that caught my eye was titled 'Saxton: Wife Beater'. I stopped dead in my tracks.

"Holy fuck! This is all my fault." I glanced around the parking lot, not exactly knowing what I was looking for but knowing I needed to find something that would give me an idea on how I could fix this.

Dom stepped up to me, tipping my head in his direction until our eyes met. "What are you talking about?"

Lifting my phone I held it out to him so he could take it.

Dom gave it one glance and rolled his eyes, shoving my phone in his pocket. He threw his arm around my shoulder and led me the rest of the way to the car. "Don't worry about that. It's a load of shit." He opened the passenger side door and I slid in, watching him walk around the car and drop into his seat.

I turned so I was facing him. "Dom, they have photos of my face. You read what they are calling you." I rubbed a hand over my temples where a headache was starting to throb. "If I'd just gone on my own or been selfish and demanded Sam come with me, Al wouldn't have been there and said you were my husband." I shook my head and regretted it instantly. "*Fuck!*" I closed my eyes as I tried to fight the pain.

Dom cradled my face and when I slowly opened my eyes I found his, inches from mine, brimming with concern. "You're hurting yourself. Please trust me when I say it's nothing to worry about." The feel of his breath against my face as he spoke had my heart beating faster.

My eyes dropped to his lips and I watched as his tongue came out to wet them, belatedly realizing mine had just done the same thing. "Do—"

I didn't get to finish saying his name because his mouth was suddenly pressed against mine, his tongue taking full advantage of my parted lips. My hand found its way into the hair at the back of his neck and as my hand moved higher I realized he must have taken his cap off. I whimpered into his mouth as his tongue danced with mine and I tugged at his hair, trying to get better access, enticing a moan from Dom.

Breaking the kiss, he pressed his forehead against mine as we both caught our breath. "I've wanted to do that for days."

His admission had my eyes popping open. "You have?"

Dom leaned back just enough for me to see his face clearly. "More than anything. Your pretty little mouth has been driving me crazy." He ran his thumb over my bottom lip.

I wanted to pinch myself. This gorgeous guy before me was speaking to me—about me—like I was something special. My insecurities started creeping in, but I batted them away. There was nothing that Dom had done since I met him that would make me doubt his word. So, swallowing down all the doubt, I crushed my lips against his in another passionate tangle of tongues, feeling sexier than I've ever felt before when he let out another moan.

CHAPTER SEVEN

DOM

THE GENTLE TUGGING on my hair had my dick hardening and my balls tightening. Needing to end the kiss before I embarrassed myself, I pulled back slightly and pressed a gentle peck against her lips before settling back in my seat, my eyes still on her face trying to work out what she was thinking. "I guess we should hit the road and you should ask me those questions."

Aimee's eyes dropped to my lips and I couldn't help but grin. I had a feeling she wanted me just as much as I wanted her. "Well, you know Google already answered most of those questions in one article," Aimie stated with a shrug.

Starting the car, I made our way out of the underground parking lot.

She let out a disappointed sigh. "Going by the pictures, I assume there was a leak at the hospital." She gasped. "I hope it wasn't Josh."

My cap slid across the dash as I took the turn out of the parking lot and Aimee reached out, catching it before placing it on her head.

"I don't know who it was but Gary is looking into it. I'm

sure he'll find out before we go back next week if that's what you're worried about."

Taking the cap off and placing it in her lap, Aimee rubbed at the left side of her head. The side on which she'd had taken the impact. Dr. Petrov had warned her about headaches, saying they were a common occurrence after a concussion.

"What should we being doing about it? Do I need to make a statement explaining the truth or should you?" she asked.

I flicked a glance at her and saw that she was biting her lip as she looked out the window, probably trying to think of ways to help me. "Aims, it'll all blow over and be forgotten when another celebrity does something the media deems more interesting."

"But Dom…" She paused, clearly thinking about her next words before saying them. "You came out of Gary's room really pissed, yet when I showed you the article you rolled your eyes. Gary had a plan, didn't he? A plan you didn't like."

I let out a sharp breath, but I wasn't at all surprised Aimee had hit the nail right on the head. She was a smart girl. "He wanted to spin it into some big hero thing. You were mugged and I saved you." I locked eyes with her for a second. "I'm not comfortable lying like that, making myself out to be a hero I'm not." I shook my head. No, that was not me. I didn't tell her the worst of it. The fact that he wanted me to paste her all over my social media, making it look like we were in love and selling the whole elopement story too. Apparently there was talk of me being in the closet since I was never seen with a male or female after the split with my ex. It had been a pretty public parting, but the reasons behind it had been kept private. There was no way I was using Aimee like that.

Never.

"Should we be addressing the fact that I'm not your wife?" she asked, her voice sounding higher-pitched than normal.

I honestly didn't know if that was a good idea or not, so I tried to explain why. "If I deny it they might just push it harder. People don't believe what they read in the papers nowadays, preferring to follow celebrities on social media instead. If I just post as normal they'll see the truth because if I had a wife, I'd surely have posted about it. My fans will know it's all crap."

Out the corner of my eye, I caught sight of Aimee rubbing her temple again.

"Why don't you close your eyes for a bit, try and sleep away that headache?" I offered. "Maybe you should take one of the pills the hospital gave you."

She screwed up her face. "Those pills make me all fuzzy in the head. I'd rather not take them if I can help it. You don't mind if I sleep?"

I waved her off. "Not at all. I'll turn the music up to drown out your snoring."

Aimee looked at me, mouth wide in shock. "I do *not* snore!"

I laughed. She was right. She didn't snore, although Aimee was a teeth grinder and sleep talker, but I wouldn't bring that up. I didn't want to keep her awake longer. Not when I could see her settling down, with her head against the window.

———

FOUR HOURS and thirty minutes later we were pulling up on my parents' drive.

Once Aimee had woken up, after having an hour-long nap, we'd played numerous games, like I-spy, a shopping basket game, and another one where when we drove past a street or a town or a creek, we had to take it in turns to come up with similar names until we decided on the most hilarious one. It was the funniest road trip I'd ever taken.

After I pulled the keys out of the ignition neither of us made a move to leave. Aimee sat looking up at our house, apprehension written in the lines on her face.

"Your family is going to hate me for all the stories floating around." She bit at her lip.

I couldn't stop myself from reaching over and flicking her lip out with the edge of my thumb. "You've already met half of my family and they adore you. They know what the press are like and won't blame you at all."

She stared at me with wide eyes. "Are you sure?"

"One hundred percent," I stated confidently.

Tempted to kiss her worries away, I leaned towards her but before I could get within reach, her door was ripped open and she spun her head around to greet my brother.

"Alberto. It's good to see you again."

"Call me Al." Al stepped back, giving Aimee room to get out. "You are looking a lot less battered than the last time I saw you."

Al hadn't seen her since the night it all happened. He'd been back to drop the car off, but I met him in the car park, needing to know where he'd parked.

Once Aimee cleared the car Al pulled her into a hug.

"Thanks, Al, I'm feeling a lot less battered and bruised too."

I climbed out of my side of the car just in time for Mom to throw her arms around me. "Hey, Mom."

"You've been away for far too long." She squeezed me tight. "I missed you."

I couldn't help but agree with her. We had been away much longer than we ever had before. Even when I went to college I was only in New York City, so I made sure to come home for weekends. "I missed you too, Mom."

Mom released me and Dad stepped up and pulled me into a manly hug with a pat on the back. "It's good to have you home, son."

"It's good to be home," I said, meaning the words wholeheartedly. There wasn't a better place to be than home, which made me question whether heading to Australia with Aimee was a good idea. I'd be away from the people I love much longer than necessary.

CHAPTER EIGHT

AIMEE

ALBERTO LET me go and a small woman with brunette hair pulled me into her arms. "Aimee, I'm so glad I'm finally get to meet you. I've heard so much about you."

I trained my worried eyes on Dom, who was hugging his Dad, while I wondered what the hell he could have told them. "It's nice to meet you too, Mrs. Saxton."

"Please, call me Rose. Mrs. Saxton is way too formal," she offered. Her hold on me lessened but she didn't let go of me completely as she directed me towards the house with an arm around my shoulder. "Come on in, let me show you where you'll be sleeping."

"My bag—" I started, while slowing our momentum.

She cut me off. "The boys will deal with that." She doubled her efforts, tugging me along the path and up the steps to the porch.

Feeling guilty that the guys were lumbered with my bags, I threw a glance over my shoulder only to find them chatting away happily as they pulled the suitcase I hadn't seen since before the hospital out of the car's boot.

Sam had packed my stuff when she'd checked out of the

hotel. Since I didn't need much while I was in a coma and during my stay, she'd packed my essentials in my duffel bag and the rest had been put in my suitcase which had—at I some point before I woke up—been put in the boot of Dom's car.

The front door opened before we got within reach, Kat stepping out and giving me a hug. Like Alberto, I hadn't seen Kat since the day of the accident so I froze as I was wrapped in her arms.

"I'm glad you're okay. Everyone was pretty worried about you." There was so much honesty behind Kat's words. My heart filled with emotion for these people who cared so much about someone who was essentially a stranger to them.

"Let's get her inside before she does a runner," Rose stated, gently shoving both Kat and me inside, a hand on each of our backs.

"Oh my god, Mom. Can you stop manhandling our guest?"

Dom's voice behind us had me turning my head to look for him, but all I saw was a blushing Rose looking back at me apologetically.

I gave her a bright smile, and then turned to follow Kat through the hallway. Glancing up at the walls I could see so many happy images of this family plastered all over them. Matt was in many of them, too, which made me realize how close Matt and Dom's friendship must be.

I paused in front of one that caught my eye. Dom had Matt in a headlock, Kat was on Alberto's back almost choking him with the grip she had around his neck and Mr. and Mrs. Saxton were watching the four of them with a lot of love in their eyes.

"That one is my favorite," Rose admitted, coming to a stop beside me.

I gave her a warm smile. "It would be mine too. There's so

much love." I stated, feeling somewhat awed at how much these people cared about each other.

"Children. No matter what trouble they're in, you can't help but love them." She shook her head disbelievingly. "What am I saying, you'll know exactly what I mean. You have your own children."

I felt my eyes widen, surprised at how much these people knew about me when we'd never previously met. A wave of worry flowed through me. Would she think less of me if she knew the trouble I had with my kids? She was right in the fact that you couldn't help but love them, no matter what. It wasn't called unconditional love for nothing. But there were days when I knew they were just total assholes. I've always said that was just teenage boys and puberty, but part of me worries it was how I'd brought them up and, perhaps, I failed in some way.

"What's the hold up? These bags aren't light," Mr. Saxton shouted behind us, saving me from having to respond.

"Dad, you aren't even carrying anything," Dom berated, the laugh behind his words making it clear he was amused.

Mr. Saxton chuckled. "I was thinking of you, son."

"Okay," Rose started as she shimmied past me. "Come, you'll be having Dom's room."

"I don't want to put anyone out. I don't mind sleeping on the couch," I offered, following her up the stairs.

"I'll have no such thing. Dominic will be fine on the camp bed in Alberto's room. Isn't that right Dominic?"

A hand brushed against the small of my back, causing a shiver to run through me as Dom stepped close. "Yes, Mom."

Rose opened the first door on the left and waved me in. "Make yourself at home. If you need any hanging space in the robe, Dominic can make some room."

My shoulders stiffened. "No, my things are fine in my suitcase. I'd probably end up forgetting things when I go home if I unpacked now." I stepped into the room, my eyes wandering over the posters on the wall and sports trophies which stood on the chest of drawers.

"Well, the offer is there if you change your mind." She gave me a warm smile. "Boys, put the bags down and let's leave Aimee to get some rest. She's probably tired."

Rose left the room, Alberto following suit with a quick wave, but Dom... Dom strode towards me like he was on a mission. His hands slipped into my hair and around my neck before I even realized he was in front of me. My back pressed against the wardrobe as Dom's mouth descended on mine. The feel of his body pressed against mine had warmth pooling inside me.

I needed to be closer.

I fisted my hands in his shirt as his tongue stroked mine in a sensual rhythm.

"Dominic Saxton! Get your behind down these stairs right now!"

Breaking our kiss with a chuckle, I rested my head against his chest as I caught my breath, letting my arms slide around his back.

His arms encased my body in a hug as we stood there, coming down from the moment. "I should really go, she'll only come and get me if I don't." I lifted my head off his chest, ready to let him step back, but caught sight of his eyes widening in terror. "And if she caught us like this...we'd never hear the end of it. She'd have the wedding planned before the end of the week."

I laughed at his words as we parted.

"You think I'm joking." He pulled a worried face and ran a hand through his hair, seeming somewhat abashed. It left me wondering whether he really believed what he'd said or was just pulling my leg.

"What is this...between us?" I slapped a hand to my

mouth in horror as I realized the question had come out of it, but before he could answer, his mom called again.

"Dominic! Don't make me come up there…"

Rose's threat had Dom pressing a quick kiss to the top of my head before stepping backwards towards the door. "We'll figure that out later. I promise." The cheeky wink he threw me as he walked out the door had my heart doing somersaults.

Feeling suddenly drained, I dropped onto the bed as the door clicked shut and rested my head on the pillow. I closed my eyes, thinking Rose may have been right in saying I needed a nap, but the minutes passed and my brain wouldn't switch off.

Deciding there was no point lying there longer, I sat up and glanced out of the window. It looked out onto the back yard that had, if my eyes weren't deceiving me, a small stream at the end and a seating area just off to one side. It looked like a soothing place.

A great place to write.

I quickly grabbed my laptop out of my bag and headed down the stairs before pausing in the hallway, belatedly realizing I had no idea how to get out there without traipsing through someone else's house.

"Can't sleep?" Rose asked, pulling me out of my concerns.

I smiled as I walked towards the open door of the kitchen where she was preparing some food. "No. My brain's not tired. I was hoping to go sit out by the stream, but I'd be more than happy to help you here if you need an extra pair of hands," I offered.

"You'll only be in my way. Go, enjoy the peace." Rose waved me off pointing to the door beside the fridge before she went back to whatever she was preparing.

As much as I would have loved to help her, she would have probably been right. I knew when I was cooking at home, if someone tried to help, they either didn't do it right or got in the way.

Being left to my own devices in the kitchen was always best.

———

THE WORDS FLOWED from my fingers while I listened to the peaceful trickle of the stream. Part of me wondered if it was the knock to the head that made it easier. If that was the case, maybe I should buy Dom a thank you basket or something. Laughter bubbled up in my chest at the thought.

A basket full of goodies and a note saying 'Thank you for knocking me out with a door'.

"What has you giggling to yourself?" Dom's voice behind me had me jumping in my seat and quickly snapping my laptop shut. "Trying to hide your words from me?"

I shook my head in answer.

He gave me a questioning look as he sat down in the chair next to mine. "You've been out here for hours, tapping away at that keyboard. Is it kinky shit? What do they call it…smut?"

My cheeks heated as I laughed. As much as I'd like to write that stuff because, hell, did it sell, I just couldn't do it. My stories always ended up on the sweeter side of things. I'd learnt to make it work and there was a market for sweet too.

He squinted, a smirk playing across his face. "You do, don't you?"

As though his smirk was infectious, I felt myself grin. "No. Honestly, I don't write smut."

"Fine, I'll believe you. Thousands wouldn't," he playfully retorted. "I would have joined you earlier, but you looked like you were in the zone and I didn't want to disturb you."

Folding my hands on top of my laptop, I gave him my full attention. "That's…Thank you."

Not many people understood 'the zone', or the flow, and how detrimental it could be to interrupt that. It made sense that Dom would get that since he was creative himself with being a songwriter. At least I thought he wrote his own songs. It wasn't something we'd spoken about.

"It was good to feel the words flowing again." The cool breeze blew a loose strand of hair into my face and I tucked it behind my ear. "This whole trip was supposed to be a writing retreat. See beautiful places, find inspiration everywhere and write. These are the first words I've written since stepping foot on American soil."

Dom gave me a knowing look. "You can plan things, but I've learnt the creative juices never stick to the plan. You've just got to sit back and wait, they'll hit you at the most surprising times."

The sun was dipping behind the trees, and when the breeze blew once again I shivered.

"You're cold. Come on, let's go inside," Dom suggested as he stood. He waited for me to stand and when I did, he tucked me under his arm, warming me with his body heat.

It felt good, being held by him.

It felt like I was right where I belonged.

Only I knew I had to leave and things between us would soon be ending. I pushed that thought to the back of my mind as I told myself I needed to live in the moment and make the most of every day I had with him.

It may hurt when it was over but I'd rather take the hurt over a lifetime of regret.

CHAPTER NINE

DOM

THE SOUND of Alberto's snoring was all wrong to my ears. It didn't matter what I did, I couldn't drift off.

Glancing at my watch I could see it was three in the morning, which meant I'd lain in bed for the last three hours staring at the ceiling.

We'd had a lovely family meal—Mom's legendary roast duck, which Aimee loved—and then spent the night having a *Beverly Hill's Cop* movie marathon. Aimee and Kat both fell asleep during the second one. *Lightweights.*

Deciding there was only one thing that would fix my problem, and let me at least get a little sleep before the neighbor's rooster started at the crack of dawn, I climbed out of the camp bed and silently snuck out of Alberto's room and along the hallway.

Gently closing the door of my room, I shut my eyes as the now familiar sound of Aimee's faint breathing reached my ears. That was what I was missing in Alberto's room…that, and the muttering she does when she dreams.

Reaching for the corner of the cover, I paused before touching it. *Should I be sneaking into her bed while she's asleep?* It was a queen, so it was more than big enough for the two of us, but…what if she didn't want me joining her?

Aimee rolled over, turning her back to me. "Get in the bed, Dom, unless you wanna be a creep and just watch me sleep all night."

An amused smile crossed my face. Aimie had woken up to find me watching her sleep a few times at the hospital. Calling me a creep for it became our little joke. It's not like I'd had much else to look at in that room; Aimee was the prettiest thing there. She'd likely be the prettiest thing anywhere.

One night I had to steal a notebook off the nurse so I could write a melody that just the sight of her sleeping form had inspired.

Her rosebud lips and freckled cheeks.

I slipped into bed behind her, shuffling until the front of my body was flush against the back of hers. My arm draping over her body so she couldn't roll away from me. Loving the feel of her in my arms as my body relaxed.

After a minute, she twisted and pressed a kiss to the center of my chest. "This feels right," she said softly. I could hear the sleep behind her words and I knew she'd fall back over within seconds.

Closing my eyes, I soon drifted off to sleep, knowing in my soul that the words she'd spoken were true. After all, I couldn't help but think we were destined.

SOFT AND TEASING fingers ran over my chest rousing me from sleep. A leg wrapped around my hip and I groaned at the friction it caused against my dick. My morning wood twitched.

Jesus!

I needed to get out of bed before I made a fool out of myself.

Aimee snuggled into me, muttering unintelligible words in her sleep. It was endearing and my pulse raced at the thought. I couldn't help but think I was falling way too fast for this woman—a woman I'd only known for a matter of weeks, and for half of that time she'd been unconscious.

Absentmindedly I ran my hand over her back eliciting a shiver. A warm smile spread across my face. It was good to know my touch affected her just as much as her touch had me. Unless, of course, she was dreaming of someone else. I quickly brushed that depressing thought away.

Her face, although resting on my chest, was turned up towards me so I watched her for a moment. Her eyes moving behind her eyelids made it obvious she was dreaming. Her breath gently blew out of her cracked open mouth and over my nipple, causing it to pebble.

I placed a soft kiss on her forehead and closed my eyes, wondering what the likelihood of falling back to sleep would be. I knew for a fact there was no chance I was getting out of this bed until Aimee kicked me out—the fact that she'd let me join her in the first place made me hopeful that she wouldn't mind me traveling with her to Australia, and perhaps staying for a while.

"Mmm… Dom. Morning." Her raspy voice had my lips turning up into a smug smile.

"You did know it was me. Does that mean I was the one you were dreaming about?" My brow rose as curiosity cursed through me.

She cracked and eye to look at me. I couldn't tell if the frown she sported was meant due to confusion, or just the brightness of the room. Her questioning word had me thinking it was the former. "Dreaming?"

"You were talking in your sleep." I smirked. "And feeling me up a little."

A pretty pink blush covered her cheeks as she buried her face in my chest with a groan. "Did I really feel you up?" she asked, her voice timid; like she wasn't really sure she wanted to know the answer.

"I'm afraid so. But on the plus side your talking was unintelligible so you at least didn't *say* anything embarrassing," I confessed, wanting to ease her mind if only just a little. "It was kind of cute."

My face heated at the admission and she chose that moment to lift her head, so I quickly turned away hoping it wasn't as obvious as it felt.

"You look pretty cute yourself when you're being all bashful." She giggled.

A fresh wave of embarrassment hit and I threw my arm over my face at an attempt to hide it. "Oh, don't. You're making it worse." I couldn't hold back a chuckle, which had her laughing harder.

Once we both calmed down, we settled back into a comfortable silence.

Running my fingertips through her dark blonde hair, I admired the softness against my skin.

Her fingers trailed around my nipple, making my dick stir.

"What is *this* between us? Are we making a mistake?" Aimee's voice was soft and tender, but I could sense the seriousness behind her questions in the way her shoulders had suddenly stiffened.

If I didn't choose my words carefully, this could all end before it even got started.

And I certainly didn't want that.

"Honestly?" She gave me a reassuring smile and I carried on. "I don't know what it is. It just feels…right." I shrugged. I quickly ran over my next words in my head and dug deep to find the courage to say them aloud. "There's been this magnetic connection between us ever since you accused me of being a hallucination."

We both laughed at the memory and the tension in Aimee's shoulders eased slightly.

"I know you probably don't feel it too. Hell, you were out of your mind and unconscious most of the time we've known each other, but I can't help what I feel. I'm falling for you." I sucked in a quick breath, amazed at my admission. "To me, feelings like that can't be a mistake."

Aimee's tear-filled eyes locked on mine as she lifted her head. I worried I'd said the wrong thing, until a small smile spread across her face. "Our lives are so different. I can only see this ending in heartbreak…but I'm willing to take all the pain in the world if it means I get to experience everything you make me feel while we're together."

Aimee raised herself up on her elbows and pressed her lips against mine. I mildly wondered if it was to stop herself from saying another word.

One word in particular.

Love.

Because as crazy as it sounded, that was the one word I'd been biting back myself. I'd lied when I'd said I was falling for her.

I was passed falling.

I was head over heels in love.

CHAPTER TEN

AIMEE

DOM'S WORDS had brought tears to my eyes and all my thoughts were suddenly falling from my mouth. Needing to shut myself up before I did something epically stupid—like saying the L-word—I crushed my lips against his.

He was soon taking control of the kiss and rolling us over so my back was pressed against the bed and he was leaning over me. Dom's tongue was stroking mine; leaving me to wish somewhere a little lower was getting stroked too.

I clenched my thighs at the onslaught of tingles that thought evoked and released a moan into his mouth.

As if Dom could read my mind his hand slid down my body, toying with the edge of my panties. He broke the kiss and locked eyes with me. "Tell me you want this?"

I nodded. *Was he crazy?* Of course, I wanted this. Shouldn't the fact that I was lifting my hips to try and maneuver his fingers closer to where I wanted them be answer enough?

"I need to hear the words, Aimee. I don't want to take this somewhere you'll regret later."

Lifting up slightly I pressed a kiss to his mouth, my teeth

tugging gently on his bottom lip for a second before releasing it. "I want it, Dom. I want you. So damn much."

The breath he released brushed over my lips before he took them in a passionate kiss, pressing me into the bed as his fingers pushed aside my panties.

Dom's fingertips gingerly skimmed over my clit and I moaned into his mouth as I forced myself not to buck against him. I needed more but I also needed him to set the pace. My ex had messed with my head in regards to sex and I'd never imagined that I'd want it again, let alone feel such desperate need for it.

Two of his fingers entered me as the heel of his palm rubbed against my clit, giving it the friction I was craving.

Within a matter of minutes my release was building—another thing that hadn't happened for me in a long time. I'd started to think I was defective.

Panic flowed through me as memories muddied my mind and I started to feel more and more out of control.

Dom bit my jaw, bringing me back to the moment. "I don't know where you've gone but you need to come back. I want to see you come. I want to feel you come on my fingers."

His words had my pussy contracting as I gave him exactly what he wanted and fell off the metaphorical cliff.

"Dom…" His name was barely a whisper, and very much a prayer, as it left my lips.

As I started to come back to my senses, I noticed Dom was leaning back and away from me. It set my insecurities off and I made a move to sit up as I tried to get out of the vulnerable position I felt I was in.

Dom smiled reassuringly, leaning over me once again and effectively halting my escape. "You look so sexy when you come."

My face flamed at his compliment but my insecurities immediately disappeared.

I took in his now naked body and couldn't quite believe I'd missed that he'd taken his clothes off until now.

My eyes ran down his body and stopped at the sight of his thick dick, which was all suited up and ready to go. The sight had me squirming eagerly on the bed. I wrapped my arms around his neck to pull him down against me.

"You like what you see?" He smirked and I knew there was no need to answer but I did anyway.

"Yes." I bit at my lip. I wanted him, but I didn't want to sound too needy by begging him to take me.

Dom ran a hand over the edge of the tank I'd slept in his fingers brushing the flesh on my stomach sent shivers over my body. "I think we need to even up the odds a little. You're not naked enough for my liking."

I stopped his hand when he'd barely moved it an inch. "Wait!"

His eyes locked on mine as he stilled and I knew he could see the panic in my wide stare.

"I'm probably not what you're used to…I've had kids. I have stretch marks and…" I paused wondering how to say what I had to say without putting him off. "My tits aren't exactly perky anymore," I blurted out as my face heated, my eyes dropping to anywhere but Dom's.

I felt his finger under my chin as he raised it. "Aims. You're beautiful. Your body, and all it's imperfections, tell a story. I can guarantee I'll have never seen something as perfect as you." He placed a gentle kiss on the tip of my nose before reaching for the edge of my tank once again.

This time I gave him no resistance. His words had wiped my worries away and I lifted slightly as the top went over my head.

Dom threw the top aside and took my mouth with his, slowly and passionately. There was no rush to his movements and it made me think he was savoring our time together.

My hips lifted of their own accord to grind against his erection and Dom pulled back from the kiss to laugh. "Keep doing that and it'll be over before we even get started."

I slid my hand between our bodies and gripped Dom's veiny cock, giving it a teasing stroke, luring a groan from him as he threw his head back in ecstasy.

Dom froze as I lined him up where I wanted him. The only thing moving being his head as he brought it down to look at me.

Our eyes connected as his tip entered me. My hand slid up his body and excitement filled me as I felt the peaks and valley's of his abs. *How did I get lucky enough to end up in bed with such a sex god?*

My fingers brushed over his nipples causing them to pebble and I couldn't help but lean forward to run my tongue over them.

As if the move spurred him on, Dom slowly eased forward, his cock deliciously inching its way in until we were pelvis to pelvis. He lowered his upper body over me but easily managed to keep the majority of his weight off me.

Being a little shorter than him meant I could I kiss across his chest and shoulders, but in no time Dom dipped his head to intercept my mouth and I let him as he slid back out of me. I released a moan into his mouth as he slammed back into me. The creaking of the bed sounded deafening, but it didn't stop him from doing it again and again.

My nails scratched across his back and the noises he gave me in return made it clear he liked it a lot, spurring me on to repeat the gesture.

He slowed his pace to leisurely, languid strokes and I felt myself nearing my climax once again.

"Aimee…" Dom breathed against my lips. The emotion I heard in my name sent me over the edge, just as I felt him reach his own climax.

Dom rolled us over, taking me with him and managing not to disconnect us. I felt self-conscious about my weight being on him, but my body felt like jelly so there was no way for me to move off him.

Dom pressed a kiss to the top of my head and I relaxed, feeling his heart beat in his chest as erratically as mine was.

As we laid in a comfortable silence, our heart rates coming down, my mind wandered.

I tried to imagine a future with us together but, no matter what changes I made in my head, I couldn't see it and in that moment, I knew what we'd just done was going to break me forever…

Because I'd just handed this beautiful man my heart and soul, knowing he was never going to be able to treasure it.

CHAPTER ELEVEN

DOM

I COULD'VE LAID THERE with Aimee in post-coital glory forever. Realistically, I knew we couldn't. For a start, my mom would be banging down the door as soon as she realized I was no longer in my little camp bed. Second, Aimee's grumbling stomach made it clear someone was ready for breakfast.

"Someone worked up a hunger," I teased.

She batted at me playfully as she shifted her body off mine. I immediately missed the feel of her against me and wished we could stay connected like that for longer.

Making quick work of removing the condom, I tied it off and threw it in the bin beside the bed.

Once I'd lain back down, Aimee rolled onto her stomach resting up on her elbows. Her fingertips ran over some of the tattoos on my arms causing gooseflesh to rise. "Some of these tatts are amazing. Do you use the same artist?"

Her question threw me for a minute, but then my eyes took in the hibiscus tattoo on her shoulder and the ones on her forearms and I realized she'd clearly found an artist she liked enough not to go anywhere else.

"No, I get one in every country I tour. It's kind of become

a little ritual." Aimee's stomach grumbled again, and my eyes moved back to her face. "Right, that's it, we have to get up and feed you."

Sliding out of bed with my back to Aimee, I reached for my basketball shorts and pulled them on.

"What about the one on your back?" she asked. "That had to have taken a couple of sessions."

She was right. It had taken three four-hour sessions. One for the outline, and another two for the shading. "Yeah, that was done in town over three long sessions. The artist, Will, he's actually by a buddy of mine from school."

Thinking about Will made me remember that I hadn't been to see him since he did it—before I signed my record deal. The memories of all the fun we used to have made me smile and I suddenly had the urge to give him a call, maybe even book in for another tattoo.

The sound of the sheets shifting made it clear Aimee was moving and, assuming she was pulling on her own clothes, I took a step away from the bed only to be pulled back with a hand snaking around my waist.

"Sit. I want to inspect it."

Looking over my shoulder I found her wrapped in a sheet, kneeling on the bed behind me, leaving enough room for me to sit comfortably on the edge. She was breathtaking to look at, and the fact that she didn't even know it made her even more beautiful.

Doing as I was told, I sat and immediately felt her hands trace the lines of the owl that I knew to be in the middle of the design.

Will and I had spoken one night about how I wanted to soar in my career. I knew the record company that was offering me a deal could help me do just that, but I also felt that if I signed the contract they would suck me dry until I'd lose myself. The next time we met he handed me the design he'd drawn and I knew I had to get it done.

It was perfect.

I also knew I had to sign the contract.

The tattoo would always be there to remind me that I could soar without losing the life I held inside me.

The owl, the skull and the flowers are all me.

Soaring, sucked dry, and full of life.

The Eye of Horus was added to provide protection.

"Your friend is good. It's so detailed."

"*Dominic!* You'd better be in that bathroom." My mom's voice echoed through the hallway and Aimee let out a giggle.

Aimee's hands dropped away and I missed the touch instantly. "Sound's like you'll have to tell me the story behind the tattoo another time, because something so intricate must have some serious meaning behind it."

Turning around, I pulled her across me, causing her to laugh before I silenced her with a passionate kiss.

Her hands slipped around my neck as she settled in my lap. I knew I should have pulled away, but...

Her taste. Her touch. Her kiss.

It was addictive and I couldn't stop myself from wanting more.

The door burst open and a gasp alerted me to the fact that it was my mother. I pulled back from the kiss but didn't loosen my hold on Aimee. "I'll be there in a minute, Mom."

She sighed unhappily, leaving the room without a word and Aimee looked at me concern in her eyes. "Is she gonna make me leave now? I know I'm probably not good enough for you an —"

"What the hell put that idea into your head?" I pressed a quick kiss against her creased brow hoping to ease some of her concern. "My mom is upset because she thinks *you* deserve better. And she's right."

Her frown intensified and I worried she'd give herself another headache. "I think you're both wrong." She climbed off my lap and sat back on the bed, pulling the sheet tighter around her body before waving me off. "Go on, you better go make it up to her."

I stood, knowing Aimee was right about me needing to go. Mom would come back if I didn't show my face downstairs soon. Leaning over, I gave Aimee a quick kiss on the top of her head before walking out of the room.

"Dom, will I be okay to have a shower before coming down?" Aimee called out before I closed the door.

I ducked my head back through the opening. "Yeah, of course. The bathroom's directly opposite."

Aimee gave me a wide smile and I closed the bedroom door, giving her privacy to throw some clothes on while she gathered her things for a shower.

I stepped into Al's room and found him sat on the bed, grinning at me. "You need to learn to be quieter, I think the neighbors heard what you two were up to."

I rubbed at the back of my neck. I may have been embarrassed but it wasn't enough to wipe the smug grin off my face. "Don't say anything to Aimee. She'd hate to know everyone heard us."

He made a show of zipping his lips and locking them before throwing the key over his shoulder. "My lips are sealed."

"Lips are sealed about what?" Kat's voice called from behind me. I stepped aside, giving her room to enter and she quickly shut the door.

Alberto shrugged making it clear he had meant what he'd said and I sighed. "If you heard…"

"You and Aimee at it like rabbits?" Kat finished for me, although I wouldn't have phrased it quite like that.

I rolled my eyes. "Yes, that. Don't let Aimee know."

She screwed up her face and I knew it was too late.

My shoulders slumped. "What did you say?" I asked, part of me thinking I probably didn't really want to know.

She shrugged. "I welcomed her to the family. Told her mom will be knitting booties now." I could feel my eyes widen at her words and she let out a laugh. "She was fine about it. She only resembled a lobster before she dashed into the bathroom.

"Oh god…" I groaned, wondering if Aimee would ever leave the bathroom after her shower.

Alberto stood and patted me on the shoulder. "She'll be fine. Mom and Dad won't say anything to her. *You* on the other hand? You'll never hear the end of it from Mom."

I sighed. He was right. It was all Mom would go on about until she found something new and exciting to obsess over. I'd have to hope Kat, Al or even Matt would do something to catch her attention. "Yeah, I know. I need to get changed before I face Mom's questions," I say before rooting through my suitcase for something to wear. Everything was clean. Mom must have washed it all when Al and Kat got home with our luggage. I'd only taken a backpack of clothes to the hospital with me, the rest I'd sent home with Kat and Al.

"I'm going go help Mom with breakfast so I can have a front row seat when you come down," Kat stated opening the door, the bounce in her step as she left gave away her excitement.

"Thanks, sis. I'll remember that next time *you're* in the bad books," I called back. Her resounding chuckle made it clear she'd heard me and didn't care.

Alberto grabbed the door before it closed. "Hey, that's a good idea. Wait for me."

I rolled my eyes while I pulled on my clothes, resigned to the fact that my brother and sister would milk the moment for as long as they could. I couldn't really blame them since it was usually those two getting into trouble with my parents, not me.

The one positive I could take out of this was at least I knew they liked Aimee and wouldn't want to make her uncomfortable by teasing her. The last thing I wanted was for my family to scare her away.

Not when I was only just winning her over.

Part of me knew I was an idiot for even thinking about a possible future between us. That part was telling me to look at it realistically and I'd easily see there was no chance for us. Aimee had said as much herself.

After all, her family was based in Australia and the likelihood of her uprooting them to move here was nonexistent, same as it was for me to relocate there.

A tiny part of me wanted to ignore all that. It had seen a glimmer of hope and was clinging onto that with everything it had. And I was rolling with it.

I didn't care that I was headed for heartbreak. In fact, I was running towards it with open arms.

THREE FULL DAYS had passed since we'd arrived at Dom's parents' house and they'd welcomed me with open arms, as if I was family. And that was before the whole house heard Dom and I together—and by together I mean having *sex*.

That first morning when Kat had 'welcomed me to the family', I thought I was going to self-combust. I'd never been so embarrassed in all my life, and that was saying something because I blush at pretty much everything.

Thankfully nobody else mentioned hearing us—not to me anyway. Dom didn't even bring it up.

I couldn't help but notice Dom had refrained from having a second round, which was starting to play on my mind. Worry coursed through me and my insecurities started speaking a little louder with each passing day.

Had I done something wrong? Maybe he thought I was shit in bed?

I wasn't concerned about him still being attracted to me. Dom made it clear he was in the way his eyes followed me around the room and in the light brushes his fingers would make over my skin whenever I was in reach.

Those little touches had me in a constant state of horniness, but when bedtime came around I'd always find myself going alone and waking up in the same empty bed. And yet, the spot next to me was always warm and covered in his lingering scent.

The fourth day was no different and my heart plummeted in disappointment as I caught sight of the empty space beside me. I sighed and couldn't help wondering if I should just book a hotel and leave. I didn't think I could survive much longer waking up to this feeling. At least in a hotel room, I'd expect to wake up alone.

A knock sounded on the door and I pulled the covers up to cover myself before calling out. I'd even resorted to sleeping topless in the hopes that it would spur him on, but had no such luck. "Come in."

Kat's head popped around the barely open door. Her platinum pixie cut styled to perfection for a rock chick. "Morning, Aims." A frown crossed her face as she caught sight of me. "Are you alright?"

Plastering a fake smile on my face, I held the sheet tighter against me. "Yeah. I'm just not a morning person," I said, not really lying because if you asked anyone that knew me they'd completely agree with that statement.

It wasn't like I was going to confide in her about Dom not wanting to have sex with me, he's her brother for god's sake. She wouldn't want to hear about that.

"I wondered if you'd like to come into town with me today?" The smile she gave me was wide and her eyes were bright, showing me that she was excited at the prospect.

The suggestion lifted my spirits a little and I smiled a genuinely this time. "Yeah, I could do with a girls' day out."

Kat grinned back. "Awesome. We could grab breakfast out; there's an amazing bakery in town."

"That sounds great," I said as I slid off the bed, being sure to keep myself covered with the sheet. "Let me jump in the shower real quick, and then I'll be down."

Kat closed the door with an excited squeal and I couldn't hold back my own excited laugh as I threw on one of Dom's shirts to wear to the bathroom.

WALKING into the kitchen I expected to find Dom waiting for me, a cup in hand, like most days but Kat was the only person there. My face fell, unable to mask my disappointment at him not being there

"Mom's gone to my Aunt's for the day; and Dom, Dad and Al have gone fishing. If we're lucky they won't catch anything and they'll be forced to bring a takeaway home."

I nodded in understanding even though I didn't really care about the takeaway thing, my mind was stuck on the fact that everyone was out except us and the devil on my shoulder was whispering again—maybe she'd only asked me out because she had nothing better to do.

Or, even worse, maybe Dom had *asked* her to keep me company.

Remembering her excitement when she asked me I brushed the paranoia away, telling myself she couldn't have been faking that. She clearly wanted to have a girls' day, whether it was her idea in the first place or not.

"Are you ready for girls' day?" I asked, as I slid my phone in my pocket and swung my handbag over my shoulder.

Grabbing her wallet off the side she dropped it in her own bag and pulled open the back door. "I sure am."

The walk into town was fresh, with the sun low in the sky and not giving off much warmth for the spring day. It was nice though. I was enjoying the fact that we didn't have to rush anywhere, which meant I could take in the beautiful scenery surrounding us.

A few people we passed clearly recognized Kat, greeting her warmly and welcoming her home. She stumbled over introducing me, obviously not knowing whether to call me Dom's girlfriend or just a family friend.

To be honest, I didn't know what I was either. Especially with Dom's weird sleeping habits the last couple of days. Was I just a friend with benefits? *Even though those benefits had fizzled out after one time together.*

As we stepped into the bakery a guy—perhaps in his early twenties—rounded the counter. "Kitty," he said as he picked Kat up and swung her around in the limited space. "We've missed you around here."

Kat laughed as he placed her back on her feet. "Only because you had to make your own coffee while I was gone."

The guy pressed a quick kiss to her cheek before taking a step back and giving her a little room. "Well, that might have played into it a little."

Kat batted at his arm playfully. "Damo, this is Aimie. Dom's…" she trailed off as she gestured towards me.

"The wife," he finished, looking me up and down a frown etched on his face, as though I was a math problem he couldn't quite work out.

My face heated under his scrutiny. "No… I'm…" I paused my correction, suddenly wondering what Dom would want me to say. It's his career and reputation at stake after all. I turned my worried gaze to Kat.

"Yeah, she's *the* wife," Kat said, taking the problem off my hands as she shook her head. "Maybe future wife, who knows?"

I coughed in disbelief at her words. "How the hell do you work that out? Our lives are worlds apart."

Damo looked from Kat to me before peering back at Kat, his brow raised in question. "Is it more serious than Sarah?"

"If you saw the way he looks at Aimee, you'd ask Sarah who?" she said, as if I wasn't even there, which made me huff in annoyance.

I knew who Sarah was. Their relationship had been all over the papers and Internet. Their split had been, too, even though most of the details had been a well-guarded secret.

A gentle hand on my forearm drew my attention to an elderly lady at my side. "You're the latest gossip, dear. You'll have to get used to people talking about you, even in front of you. That's just what small towns are like."

I gave her a small smile and thanked her for the advice before she walked over to the counter to pay her bill, leaving me just as swiftly as she came.

"Aims, what drink do you want? Damo will make it while we decide which yummy pastry we're going to eat with it."

Laughing, I let my eyes drift over the pastries and within seconds I knew exactly which one I wanted. "I'll have a cappuccino, please, and I don't need time to choose a pastry. I'll have one of those cinnamon scrolls," I said pointing to the glaze covered deliciousness behind the glass. "Thank you."

"Good choice. Coming right up." Damo moved away without even asking Kat what she'd like. Behind the counter he pulled two cups down and started working the coffee machine.

Kat grabbed my wrist and tugged me towards an empty table. My bum had barely touched the seat before she jumped in with the tough questions.

"So, what's going on with you and Dom? I can't help but notice he's been acting weird the last few nights."

I was in two minds how to feel about her admission. I was relieved to know it wasn't all in my head, but that also invoked a sinking feeling in the pit of my stomach because it meant it *was* something…

Something *big* if she'd noticed too.

I shrugged. "I don't know. I think…maybe he's not interested in me in that way anymore and doesn't know how to tell me." I pinned her with a questioning stare. "Should I confront him and tell him it's okay? That I get it?"

She took in a sharp breath as her eyes widened in surprise. "You seriously think he's not interested? He's more than interested, Aimee. I can promise you that."

"Here we go," Damo said as he placed a tray on the edge of the table. "One cappuccino and a cinnamon scroll for the beautiful newcomer." I blushed at his compliment as he placed my items in front of me before doing the same for Kat. "And an apricot pastry with a hazelnut latte for pretty Kitty."

"You know, Damo, compliments won't get a tip from me." Kat poked out her tongue and he quickly mirrored the gesture, causing me to giggle at their antics.

I watched him walk back to the counter before gazing back at Kat. "You and Damo…? Is there something there?" I fished for information, thinking I had to be onto something. They were so playful and flirtatious.

Kat laughed. "No," she denied. "I need someone who'd want to commit to an actual relationship, and Damo is a player. Such a player he'll go for anything with a pulse."

I watched him flirting with another customer and couldn't help but think she might've been labeling him wrongly. I didn't know the guy but watching him now, it was clear he wasn't serious when he flirted with the other customers. He was just putting a smile on his customers' faces and hopefully making them feel a little special. The way he'd been acting with Kat had been completely different; there'd been warmth there.

I didn't bother arguing with her because maybe I was the

one in the wrong and their friendship was what made it so different. Either way, I had a feeling it would all be laid out in time.

"What's the plan for the rest of the day?" I asked, even though the burning questions on my tongue were more focused on Dom. I wanted her to tell me what she meant with her promise, but had no idea how to bring up the subject again.

Kat gave me a nervous glance. "Actually, I'm thinking of getting another tattoo. Would you mind coming with me? It won't take long, it's just some song lyrics that I'm after."

Excitement bubbled up inside me. I loved going into tattoo studios, they have this vibe about them. I can't even describe it. The sound of that needle buzzing is like music to my ears, although I know I'll end up leaving the place planning my next tattoo. "Are you kidding me? I'd love to go with you. I might even see if he can book me in for one while I'm here."

"That's great. Will is amazing, I'm sure he'll be happy to fit you in."

The name sounded familiar and I creased my brow to help me remember where I'd heard it before. "Will? Is that the same Will that did Dom's back piece?"

Kat's mouth turned up in a wide grin. "Yes. That tattoo is epic. I wish I was brave enough to get a big statement piece like that."

"It is such a beautiful piece," I admitted, still wondering what the story was behind it. The fact that Dom wouldn't allow himself to be left alone with me meant we hadn't really had a chance to talk about stuff like that.

God did I miss those intimate chats.

Like the ones we'd had in the late hours of the night at the hospital.

I suddenly found myself wishing I'd never been discharged from the hospital.

————

A LITTLE BELL above the door rang as Kat pushed her way into the tattoo studio, causing a woman behind the counter to look up as we walked in. "Kat!" She cried excitedly. In one quick move, she rounded the counter and threw her arms around Kat.

"Kelsey." The thrilled tone in Kat's voice and the way they squeezed each other tightly told me they were more than familiar with each other. I wondered if they'd been life long best friends.

As they hugged it out, I took in the stunning woman with long auburn hair scraped back into a ponytail. Kelsey had an eyebrow piercing, as well as a row of earrings up her ear that were almost identical to Kat's. There were some visible tattoos on her arms but she wasn't completely covered in them, not like you'd expect of someone who worked in a place like this. Just a handful of small ones that I guessed all had a reason to be there.

As they parted Kat gestured towards me. "Kels, this is Aimee."

"Ooh, so this is who's caught Dom's eye." She gave me a quick wave. "Nice to meet you, Aimee."

I felt my eyes widen in surprise at her remark. I couldn't believe everyone seemed to know about me when there really wasn't anything notable happening between Dom and me.

I waved back, feeling slightly lame. "Hi."

A tall and handsome blond guy, who looked to be in his late twenties, stepped out of a back room. "I thought I heard my next customer," he stated as he leant against the doorframe, his arms crossed over his chest and a wide smile on his face.

Kat's back straightened and she grinned in his direction "You heard right. Are you ready for me, Will?"

Will smirked. "That's a loaded question, Kat."

Her face turned a lovely shade of pink. "I…that's…not what I meant." I watched her eyes flick to Kelsey's as she absentmindedly twisted a ring on her finger.

Kelsey's eyes were staring of into the distance and it was hard to tell whether she'd even heard the exchange between the others. Kat's shoulders seemed to relax at the sight before she trained her eyes back on Will.

"Don't worry yourself, Kat. Come on." He waved her into the room he'd come from. "Is your friend coming in too?" he asked.

Kat gave me a wary look. "If that's okay with you?"

"I'm not going to say no to the company of two pretty ladies." He threw me a wink and, feeling my own cheeks heat, I ducked my head hoping to hide it. The chuckle I heard from him as I passed told me I'd failed miserably.

As I followed Kat I mentally berated myself. How come I always ended up being such a fool when it came to cute guys being nice to me?

It wasn't like he'd been coming on to me, he was just being friendly. I wouldn't even be interested if he were because he wasn't Dom. Plus, I'd be heading home within the next few days—providing the doctor gave me the okay. *Dear God, I hoped he would.* I did feel perfectly fine apart from the odd migraine.

The thought of going home gave me mixed emotions. I was so looking forward to seeing my family, but it was going to be hard saying goodbye to the new friends I'd made here.

And Dom.

Saying goodbye to Dom was going to break me.

CHAPTER THIRTEEN

DOM

I WALKED in the door expecting to find Kat and Aimee watching some chick flick but the house was dark and empty. Granted, we'd stayed out a little later than normal but Kat knew we'd be coming home with dinner, whether we caught it or not.

As I switched on the light and headed to the kitchen, I pulled out my cell to check for messages, and seeing no notifications I called out to Al. "Hey Al, have you heard anything from Kat?"

It was a second before he replied, and I guessed he'd been checking the screen of his own cell. "No, but I'll give her a call."

"No girls?" Dad asked as he made his way into the mudroom to put the fishing gear away.

I shook my head, even though he couldn't see me, and placed the bag of food on the table. "No. Al's ringing Kat now to see where they are."

Al entered the kitchen, his eyebrows drawn in a puzzled look. "She's not picking up. Why don't you try Aimee?'

I ran my hand through my hair, feeling somewhat stupid. "I don't have her number."

Al's frown intensified. "What? How do you not have your girlfriend's cell?"

"We've been in each other's company pretty much twenty-four-seven since she woke up from her coma." I shrugged sheepishly. "I haven't exactly needed it."

Dad patted me on the back. "Don't worry yourself, I'm sure they'll be fine."

Ignoring the food, I paced the small kitchen. "What if something's happened? Some complications from Aimee's accident?"

"Jesus, Dom, you are such a worry wart. She hasn't had any problems since well before she left the hospital. She'll be fine." Al stated as he started pulling the food out of the bag. "And besides, Kat would call you if that was the case." Regardless of Al's words, worry coursed through me.

I dialed Kat's number and when it went to voicemail, I called again. After the third try she answered.

All I could hear was background noise.

"Kat? Are you there?"

The background noise died down and Kat's laugh rang through the line. "Dom! Hey! Did the fish bite? Shit…what time is it?" Her words were slurred, making me think she'd been drinking.

"Yeah. We're home and you're not. Where are you guys?" I asked as my worry started multiplying. *Was Aimee even with Kat?*

I mentally kicked myself; of course she would be.

"Bronco Jack's," she said, naming the local honkytonk. We might play your everyday chart music but we were brought up with country music. Many of our early songs were country; they just weren't the songs that shone on our demo according to our manager, Gary.

We hoped down the line we'd be able to get back to our country roots. For the time being, we'd stick with what Gary shaped us into.

"Is Aimee okay? The music isn't giving her headaches or anything?"

"No, she's fine. She's dancing with Will. If she was having headaches we'd have gone back home." She paused before going on. "We've already eaten. If you guys have anything left we'll warm it up for lunch tomorrow. Don't wait up for us."

My brain was stuck on the words *she's dancing with Will*, so by the time the rest of her words caught up with me and the line was quiet in my ear, I belatedly realized she'd disconnected the call.

"The girls alright?" Dad asked around a mouthful of his fish. We hadn't caught anything big enough to bring back and cook so we'd stopped off at a takeaway and ordered fish and chips for us all. It's what we usually did when we went fishing.

"Yeah." I rubbed at the back of my neck, trying to release some tension that had built up. "They're at Bronco Jack's."

"That's good. So, why is your frown even worse than it was when you didn't know where they were?" He placed his fork on his plate, giving me all his attention.

I sighed. "Because Aimee's dancing with Will."

I knew Will had no issues attracting the girls and I was certain he'd pile on the charm with Aimee. After all, she was just his type. I knew because she was mine and we were always fighting over girls back in the day. I couldn't help but wonder if he'd be hers?

"Oh my god… You're jealous! I never thought I would see the day that Dom Saxton would be hit with the jealousy bug!" Al was fist-pumping the air in excitement, making me roll my eyes.

Grabbing the truck keys off the hook where Dad had

hung them I headed for the door, knowing I wouldn't feel better until I could see what was happening with my own eyes.

"Wait up there!" Dad called, halting my steps with his command. I may be an adult, but if my father tells me to do something, I do it. "At least eat your food first. There's no point starving yourself when the girls are perfectly fine."

I didn't move as I contemplated my next course of action. They might be perfectly fine but Aimee was dancing with a guy who'd most definitely be making moves on her, and I hadn't even kissed her today.

What if she thought I wasn't interested?

I'd been avoiding her since everyone heard us having sex, not wanting to give anyone a reason to embarrass her if something like that happened again.

"Dom. Eat!"

I sighed at Dad's demanding tone but still; I turned and sat at the table.

Dad pushed a plate of food over having already dished up my serve and I tucked in, knowing he was right. It'd be ridiculous to rush out after Aimee without eating, especially when they could have been with Will for hours and if he were going to make a move he would have by now. I'd just have to deal with whatever may or may not have happened when I did eventually get there.

Dad was watching me intently, so I didn't rush my food because I knew he'd only berate me if I did. When I was finished I took my plate over to the sink and quickly washed it, placing it on the draining board as Al stepped up beside me.

"You alright?" He asked as he washed his plate.

I grunted in reply, grabbing the keys off the table where I'd left them and headed for the door once again. "Catch you later, Dad."

"I know you're worried about your girl, but make sure your sister gets home safe, too."

I looked over my shoulder locking my eyes on his. "Of course," I promised, unable to believe he'd think otherwise. Me, Al, and even Matt had always been protective of Kat—she'd more than likely say overly so—just because I had an interest in a girl didn't mean I'd forget all about my sister.

He gave me a grateful smile in return and waved towards the door. "Go. Have fun."

"Hey, wait for me." Al called as I strode to the truck. "I'm not missing out on seeing you go all caveman…against Will Sibree, of all people."

I shook my head. Yeah, Will might've been a hard ass, having spent some years on the fighting circuit, but that didn't mean we'd be fighting. For a start, I didn't plan on going in there all caveman like anyway.

CHAPTER FOURTEEN

AIMEE

A SLOWER COUNTRY song came on and Will pulled me into his arms, instantly swaying me around the floor like a pro. I've always had two left feet, but he moved us around so gracefully I was sure it even made me look good. It left me pondering whether he'd ever danced professionally.

When Will first offered to dance, I'd worried he'd try grinding against me like guys often did but he'd been nothing but a gentleman. He'd taught me some line dances as the rest of the dance floor broke out in them, and then as the slower songs came on he'd pulled me close but didn't encroach on my personal space by holding me at just the right arms' length.

"What's going on in that pretty little head of yours? I can almost see the cogs going around." His lips brushed against the shell of my ear as he spoke.

I pulled back a little to look in his sky blue eyes and couldn't help but notice how handsome he was as he gave me a raised brow. I leaned back in towards him so I could speak into his ear—otherwise he'd have no chance of hearing me over the music. "I was wondering if you'd ever had dance classes or something."

Will threw his head back and laughed loud enough to cause a few people around us to stare.

My face heated with the attention and I buried my face against his chest, the cotton of his black shirt soft against my skin. His cologne was a pleasant scent, but it wasn't Dom's and I suddenly wished he were here dancing with me.

After Will calmed down and his chest stopped jumping with laughter, I felt his lips brush against my ear again. "No, I can't say I've ever had a dance lesson. I guess I'm just a natural. It's probably the country boy genes."

I felt him loosen his hold on me and lifted my head in question, to find Dom standing beside us. My eyes widened in surprise as I wondered how he even knew we where we were. I watched as Dom said something to Will, my eyes unable to make out the words as his lips moved.

Will smirked and patted Dom on the shoulder before pressing a quick kiss to my cheek. "If Dom doesn't move as well, you can find me at the bar."

I laughed as he walked away and my eyes fell on Dom who was holding out his arms for me. I stepped into them without question, breathing in the familiar scent of his cologne as I rested my head against his chest, finally feeling like I was where I belonged.

"Aims…" My name fell from his lips so quietly that I doubted he even meant to say it aloud.

I lifted my head and reached up to speak into his ear. "I missed you today," I said, not feeling at all ashamed to admit it.

Dom pressed a kiss to my lips, titling his head just right to make sure we didn't knock his cap off. "You won't believe how happy those words make me. I missed you too."

The song changed to a more upbeat one and Dom's movements stopped. I reluctantly stepped back as Dom's hands fell away from me. I wanted to beg the band to play something less upbeat, just so I could be close to Dom. I'd not been kidding when I'd said I'd missed him. In fact, I'd missed touching him and here, on the darkened dance floor, it felt intimate being so close.

It was an intimacy I'd craved for days.

Dom's hand slipped into mine and I lifted my eyes to his. He nodded his head in the direction of the bar and I smiled. Now that I'd thought about the bar I was starting to feel parched. I'd been dancing with Will for a long time and we hadn't even paused for a drink.

We came to a stop at a tall table and as Dom wrapped his arm around my waist pulling me into his side, Will handed me a bottle of water.

"I figured you'd need this," he said without needing to raise his voice too much since the music was a little quieter away from the dance floor.

I smiled gratefully. "Thanks, Will." I unscrewed the top and took a good gulp of the cool liquid.

"Where's my sister?" Dom asked, as his eyes flicked around the bar.

I let my eyes roam the dance floor in search of her. Most of the time we'd been out there dancing Kat hadn't been far. She'd been happily dancing with Kelsey and whichever guys tried to get close to them. Not that either of them paid any attention to the poor guys.

At the bakery I'd wondered why Kat was so insistent that Damo wasn't for her but seeing her with Kelsey made me realize exactly why.

Kat was interested in someone else.

Kelsey.

She hadn't wanted to tell me she was a lesbian, and I understood why. Kat hardly knew me. Hell, I didn't even know if anyone else knew and I certainly wouldn't say anything unless she did.

"Dom?" Kat's voice came from behind us and we all spun around to face her. "What are you doing here?"

"He came to be all caveman and claim his girl." Alberto stepped up beside them giving me a brief smile before smirking smugly at Dom. "Don't deny it, Dom. You were jealous when you heard Aimee was dancing with Will."

Dom stiffened next to me and my eyes floated over him. He had a visible tick in his jaw. "Fine. Yes, I was jealous. But I didn't go all caveman." He sighed, losing some of the tension in his shoulders. His eyes moved from me to Will. "Did I?"

Even though he wasn't addressing me I shook my head in answer. I hadn't witnessed him doing anything cavemen like.

"Hmm… Now that you mention it, when you told me I was dancing with your wife all that was missing was the fists beating on your chest," Will stated, making the others laugh.

I looked at Dom wide-eyed. "Seriously Dom? If you don't stop calling me that people won't believe it's just a rumor."

Dom shrugged. "I don't care what they think. I quite like saying it."

I caught sight of Alberto giving Dom an expressive stare.

"I need a drink," Al stated as he walked away shaking his head.

Will pierced us with a questioning look. "So, you guys aren't actually married?" He sounded genuinely intrigued.

A frown creased my brow. "We've known each other for less than a month, of course we aren't." My eyes roamed between the others.

Kat and Kelsey both gave Dom a meaningful look I couldn't quite place, it left me worried. *Did they know something I didn't?*

Dom stumbled forward as someone bumped into him.

"Sorry," a female voice said absently as we turned to look at her. She lifted her head and visibly paled recognition clear on her face.

"Holy shit! You're Saxton." Her eyes flicked between us and brightened even more. "And Kat." She looked around obviously looking for someone, but with one last nervous glance at Dom she ran off towards the dance floor without another word.

"Well, that could have been worse," Kat stated with a shrug.

"I've just been informed that we have a special guest here tonight," a voice called over the speakers.

Dom groaned beside me. "You were saying?" he said, giving Kat a regretful look.

"Running Hearts are in the house. How about you give them a warm welcome and they might even jump on stage to give us all a song for old times sake," the voice on the speaker stated confidently.

I watched Dom's shoulders fall in defeat as he and Kat seemed to have a conversation with a look. He turned to face me, a grim gaze taking away his usual spark. "We're going to have to do it. Do you mind?"

I gave him a wide smile. "You're forgetting I missed your last concert." I stepped in close and undid an extra button on his shirt—knowing the fans would love seeing a peek at his chest tattoos—before I patted him. "Go. Put on a good show."

As I made a move to step back, his hands snaked around my waist and he pulled me closer so there was no room between us. His mouth was suddenly on mine, causing me to lose myself as I melted into him and closed my eyes, opening up at the swipe of his tongue.

Dom ended the kiss too soon for my liking but I didn't cling on, even though my body wanted me to. He stepped back and gave me a brief smile. "I won't be long."

Kelsey grabbed my hand as Dom and Kat headed off towards the stage. "Lets go find somewhere we'll have a good view. They're amazing when they do these intimate events."

Once we'd found the perfect spot at the side of the dance floor, Alberto stepped up beside us. I watched Dom and Kat chat to the singer from the other band—who had most probably been the one to invite them on stage—like they were old friends.

"You should be careful how you two act in public," Alberto said into my ear, leaning in close to be heard. "You never know who might be watching and recording on their cellphones."

His finger came into my line of sight, pointing out a number of girls on the dance floor. All with their phones directed at Dom on the stage. A couple of girls here and there were talking, heads close together, their eyes shifting to me every few seconds making it clear they were talking about me and had most probably seen the kiss. Hell, it could be on one of their phones.

"Shit! I see what you mean." I gave him a sideways glance and a grateful smile. "Thank you."

"Hello," Dom's voice called through the microphone. "We hadn't planned on performing tonight so we're not exactly prepared." His eyes seemed to take in the audience as though he was addressing every individual.

"Unfortunately, Matt isn't with us tonight," he admitted, his voice sounded wary and I guessed that it wasn't often they performed without the whole band being present.

Groans of complaint flit around the crowd at his admission.

He waved a hand in the air dismissively. "Don't worry, I've got the perfect replacement with me. I even have someone to play the keys, too."

"Oh, fuck no!" Will's outburst had me turning my attention to him as he stood a few steps away from me.

"Will. Al. How about it guys?" Dom carried on, obviously not hearing Will's complaints through the crowd. "My buddy,

Will, often played guitar with me and Matt back in high school. And my brother Al is a genius on the keys. Come on guys, where are you?"

Dom looked out towards the table he'd left us at. Squinting against the lights, clearly not being able to see a thing through them. "Will…Al…"

Al handed me his glass, which smelled like bourbon, before setting off for the stage. He pinned Will with a meaningful stare as he passed. "If I have to suffer this so do you."

I nudged Will with my elbow. "You better go."

"She's right," Kelsey said from his other side. "You know Dom will only come down here and drag you up there if you don't."

"Fuck! You're right." He downed his drink before passing the empty glass to Kelsey and heading off towards the stage. Judging by the tension in his shoulders, you'd think he was walking to his death.

Dom patted Will on the back once he'd made it on stage and said something, enticing a nod from him.

A guy from the other band handed Will a guitar and he stepped to the right hand side of the stage. Kat was already behind the drums at the back and Al was ready behind the keyboard to the left.

Dom had his back to the crowd as he nodded his head, most probably counting down. After three sharp nods, he spun around and stepped up to the microphone stand, completely in the persona of Saxton.

As the others started playing a country rhythm on their instruments, he opened his mouth and a soft country song—one I'd never heard before—came out. It surprised me because the songs they normally performed were pop rock.

But watching them on that stage and seeing how relaxed Dom was singing country made me think *this* was where his heart really belonged.

CHAPTER FIFTEEN

DOM

"THANK YOU, AND GOOD NIGHT," I called into the microphone before taking a quick bow and walking off the stage. I didn't get far before a few girls accosted me for autographs and selfies. It's something I don't normally mind doing but I'd already left Aimee long enough, having sung five of our old songs.

"Come on ladies, let the man get back to his friends. I think he's given you enough of his time tonight," Zac, the lead singer from the other band, called out over the mic.

The girls dropped away without argument and Kat slipped her arm into mine, tugging me in a different direction to the one I'd been heading in.

"They moved for a better view when we headed for the stage," she explained, addressing the puzzled look I was giving her.

I didn't know how she'd seen them when I hadn't, since we'd both been blinded by the spotlights, but I took her word for it.

We came to a stop at the side of the dance floor and spotting Aimee, I stepped towards her ready to pull her into my arms. They felt empty without her there.

A worried look crossed her face and she gave me a small smile before sidestepping me. "Al. Here's your drink," she said passing him a glass as he stepped up behind me. "It's probably watered down and warm now since the ice has melted but…"

"Thanks, sweetheart. I appreciate it."

My brows furrowed at his term of endearment, as I wondered when they'd had the chance to get so close. I reached out to catch Aimee's hand in mine, but Alberto shook his head before making a show of glancing around. My eyes followed his, but all I saw were fans sneaking glances our way. Some had cellphones held up in their hands, obviously taking photos or videos.

Photos or videos.

That's what Al's trying to tell me. Why didn't I think of that sooner?

Jesus.

It's one thing kissing her when I was incognito, but to be affectionate after my cover was blown, when everyone had their eyes and cellphones on me? That was asking for trouble for her, and it would give Gary exactly what he'd wanted. I wasn't willing to do that when he'd suggested it and nothing had changed my opinion on that.

I mouthed a 'thanks' to him as I listened to Kat telling Will how awesome he was.

"You were fantastic, Will."

"She's right. Thanks for coming up with us," I said, needing to let him know I actually did appreciate it.

Will let out a nervous laugh. "Like I had much of a choice." He glanced down at his hands and shook them out. "My hands are still shaking."

Al patted him on the shoulder. "You hid it well on stage."

"I was alright on stage, my hands were busy." His blue eyes locked onto mine. "Thank you for singing those old songs. If you'd done any of your new stuff I'd have been fucked."

I shrugged. "Those songs are our roots, and anyway I'm pretty sure our newer stuff wouldn't have gotten a very good reception here. We're in a honkytonk after all."

Groups of girls kept edging their way closer to us. You could tell by the whispers and little shoves they gave one another they were daring each other to approach me.

A pretty brunette—who was under twenty-one going by the underage stamp on her hand—must have been the brave one. As she stepped forward, barging Aimee out of the way, she ran her eyes up and down Al's body before doing the same to both Will and me.

"Which one of you is going to buy me a drink?" she asked.

She definitely had some balls.

I watched Aimee shuffle around behind her, making her way towards Kat and Kelsey.

Only Kat didn't stay where she was. She edged forward until she was face to face with the brunette. "Look, sweetheart. You tried, and I totally give you an A plus for that, but there are three guys and three girls here. It's just rude to expect them to dump us for you."

"Two of them are your brothers," the girl stated correctly, making it clear she knew who we were before tonight.

Al ran a hand through his hair, obviously not liking the tension between Kat and the brunette. He'd always hated confrontation and avoided it whenever necessary, that was one of the reasons he wasn't a full member of the band. He liked being able to hide in the shadows.

"Well then, obviously you know who I'm going home with. Right, handsome?" she asked, drawing my attention again as she stepped up to Will, wrapping her arms around his neck and all but climbing him.

His face flamed, but he played along. "Can't wait, babe." He leaned in close to her and I thought I was going to have to punch my pal for kissing my sister. Instead of locking lips, he rubbed his nose against hers before running it across her cheek before nuzzling in the crook of her neck. It looked like he was kissing her but I was pretty sure he wasn't.

At least I hoped he wasn't.

The brunette huffed and stormed off back to her friends.

I straightened my cap, feeling ready to take the damned thing off. "Let's call it a night. We're not going to be able to relax here now."

The others nodded in agreement, and Kelsey headed for the door. Kat and Will following her hand in hand, still playing to their lie. Aimee fell into step behind them and as much as I wanted to join her, pick up her hand, I didn't.

"That was good thinking of Aimee," Alberto said, leaning over my shoulder as we followed the others.

"What was?" I gave him my back, turning my head slightly and hoping my words made it to him over the music. We stepped outside and I turned to face him, noticing the others stopping a little further up the road. "What was?" I repeated.

He rolled his eyes. "Kat and Will… Aimee was going to do it but she worried if the girl had seen you two earlier she'd know she was lying. And she couldn't do it with you because…well, that would be stupid for it's own reasons."

"Huh." I give him a stunned look. I'd just assumed it was Kat's idea; it seemed like something she'd come up with and I'd not even seen Aimee and Kat talking. Not that that was surprising, I'd been focused on Al. I bit at the side of my cheek as I contemplated what was going around in my head and how best to word it. "Would it be such a bad idea to go public with Aimee?"

Alberto gave me a solemn stare. "If you do, what will happen when you come back to the US and leave her in Australia?"

I shrugged. I didn't want to think about that.

I didn't want to leave her.

Ever.

He sighed. "The press will hound her. Your fans might even stalk her, either because they'll idolize her or hate her. Her life will be turned upside down. And it won't be just her. It'll be her kids too."

Pulling my cap off my head, I folded it before shoving it in my back pocket and ran my hand through my hair to get some air to my head. "Shit. You're right. I need to make an announcement and end the wife rumors." I'd been so selfish, not even considering the fact that it wasn't just Aimee. There were three kids that would be affected as well.

Al's eyes widened in surprise. "Gary won't agree with it."

I fished the truck keys in my pocket. "No. But if I post a video on social media he can't do anything about it."

A grin spread across Alberto's face and I could only imagine how it mirrored my own. "Yes. That'll work." Al seemed happier than he had in days and I gave him a wary look.

"Is this the reason you've been off with me?"

"I guess." Al shrugged his shoulders. "She's a nice girl and doesn't deserve the shit she'll get if her name's out there. The media and all the crap that comes with it is one of the things I really hate about this life." His dark eyes bored into mine as he confirmed what I'd already known about his reasons for not being in the band. "Don't you wish you could have a normal life back sometimes?"

His question is one that has crossed my mind great deal

lately. Especially when I was sat alone in the dark listening to the machine breathe for Aimee. I pondered it a lot during those dark hours. "Yeah, I have. But this life does have a lot of good points too."

He smiled sadly. "I know. But no matter what happens between you two, she'll never get to truly experience most of them."

I nodded, knowing exactly what he was thinking about. Those times when we're on stage and the crowd sings back the songs to us. Or the moment the lights hit the stage and they get their first look at us. The excitement that runs through those thousands of people…

That excitement is like a living force; you feel it in your soul.

"Are you two coming or not?" Kat called, clearly sick of waiting for us.

I glanced over to her, giving Al a nudge with my elbow. "We better go before she makes us regret even coming out tonight."

Al's face morphed into a look of worry. "You're right." We both sped up just to make sure we got there quickly so I could point out the truck and get her home before she came up with a cunning plan.

———

IT DIDN'T TAKE us long to get home — after we'd all managed to squeeze into the truck, that is.

Will, being the biggest out of him and Al, rode shotgun while the other four squeezed in the back. Aimee sat on Al's knee and I gritted my teeth, not liking it one bit. I did offer Al the keys but the bastard had had a couple of drinks and we'd been brought up knowing not to drink and drive. Luckily, Will didn't live too far away and once we'd dropped him off

Al took his seat. Kelsey was next and then it was a straight run home.

We found dad scrolling through his cellphone with a muted game playing on the TV. We all dropped onto the large lounge.

"I see you got talked into performing," he stated, not taking his eyes off his cell.

I frowned as the others gave me equally puzzled looks. "How the hell do you know that?"

Dad held up his cell although he didn't need to, the sound coming out of it told me enough. It was my voice, singing Wicked Love, one of the songs I'd sung tonight. "It's had thousands of views." He dropped his cellphone back in his lap, stopping the video. "One of the other songs has even more." He turned in his seat to look at us. "Not to mention that kiss."

"Kiss?" Aimee blanched and I watched Alberto try to console her by giving her forearm a gentle squeeze.

"Yep. Going by the comments the fans are pretty obsessed with our Aimee already. Trying to work out who she is. There was talk of her being an actress from some show, Pretty Little…something," Dad admitted as he screwed up his face in thought.

"Liars. Pretty Little Liars, Dad," Kat offered and Dad shrugged, clearly not caring what the show was called.

My cell rang and I didn't need to see the name on the screen to know it was Gary. I pulled it out of my pocket and lifted it to my ear as I headed out of the house and on to the back veranda for some privacy.

"Hello."

"Saxton. You did just want I wanted and the songs…the fans are loving the new sound." The excitement in Gary's voice was palpable.

I rolled my eyes. "You hated those songs when I sent you our demo. You said they wouldn't get us anywhere."

"No...I..." He cleared his throat. "Well, I'm man enough to admit that I was wrong."

"And the other thing wasn't anything to do with what you wanted," I said, wanting to make it clear that I wasn't using Aimee the way he'd wanted me to. Hell, I was planning on clearing the wife shit up via a live video. I just had to work out how too explain that kiss. Not that I'd warn him about any of that. I wouldn't put it past him to make his own announcement first if he was aware of my plans.

I heard him sigh down the line.

"Regardless of whether you meant to or not, it still worked perfectly to what I had in mind. So, good job." I heard a noise in the background and he paused for a minute as if he was giving someone else his attention. "Look, I'm going to have to go. I was just ringing to tell you to write more of what you sang tonight. I want that to be the direction of your next album. Keep up the good work."

The line cut off before I could reply and I stared out into the darkness of the backyard as I slipped my cell into my pocket while contemplating what I could do to keep the attention off Aimee.

Alberto was right about this having the ability to ruin her life, not to mention her family's.

I couldn't let that happen.

Ever.

CHAPTER SIXTEEN

AIMEE

AFTER GIVING Dom a few minutes of privacy for his phone call, I made an excuse about needing a glass of water, so I could leave the room.

Once I was in the kitchen I stood over the sink watching Dom out the window.

He'd finished his phone call, and was leaning over the verandah railing, his shoulders slumped in defeat. Whatever his conversation had been about, it couldn't have been good.

Feeling a sudden urge to comfort him I made my way outside. "Hey," I said, wanting to alert him to my presence, before briefly sliding my hand up his back as I came to a stop beside him.

Dom gave me a brief smile before turning to look back out at the yard.

I didn't break the silence. Instead, I stared out into the darkness myself, giving him the time and quiet he clearly needed to work through whatever was plaguing his thoughts.

"That was Gary," he started, still staring out into the night. "He was congratulating me on the new songs. Songs he thought were shit when he signed me up." He forced out a laugh.

I opened my mouth to speak but he carried on.

"He also told me well done for the kiss." He turned his body to face me, so I in turn faced him, leaning my hip against the railing. His eyes were pleading with me, but I had no idea what he was pleading for. "He thought I'd done what he wanted and orchestrated it for the cameras. He'd wanted me to use you for publicity. That was what he'd suggested that day in the office."

My heart sank with his words.

Had all this between us been a lie? Just something his manager told him to do?

Our first kiss had been right after leaving the office. Maybe it had all been for Gary.

My eyes filled with tears and I couldn't tell if they were from anger or sadness because I was suddenly filled with both.

"Aims, whatever you're thinking you're wrong." The pitying look he gave me chased my sadness away and made my anger double.

"Then do tell, what exactly should I be thinking?" I snapped as I took a step backwards, needing more space between us.

Dom ran a hand through his hair. A gesture I was getting familiar with, something he did when he was frustrated. "You're doubting everything that's happened between us and you shouldn't. It's real. So *fucking* real." His eyes once again locked on mine and what I saw in them had me unable to look away. "I know the minute you walk out of my life, I'm done for. My heart, well and truly destroyed."

My heart soared with his words, but as much as I wanted to believe them a small part of me still worried he was just playing me.

"I know it's a lot, asking you to trust me but…" he started as though he could read my mind.

Dom stepped forward, reached out and wiped an escaped tear from my cheek. "I'm in love with you, Aimee. *Madly* in love with you."

As the words registered in my mind I took in the sight of him. His dark hair mussed from his frustrated ministrations. The fierce, almost demanding, sparkle in his eyes as if he was willing me to believe his words. Deep down, I knew I could believe him because he'd done nothing to make me doubt his word. Yes, he may have been off with me since we'd had sex, but I didn't doubt the sexual attraction between us.

There was nobody watching us in his bedroom that morning so there'd be no reason to fake that.

I dropped my eyes to his lips as I stepped closer to him, eliminating the space between us. "Madly in love?" I asked, feeling a small smile turn the corner of my mouth.

Dom pressed a gentle kiss to the tip of my nose. "Truly."

He moved to my chin. "Madly."

"Deeply," he said as he brushed my lips with his. He went to pull back but I halted his escape by wrapping my arms around his neck as I crushed my lips against his.

I wanted to show him the feeling was mutual. I didn't want to just say it, because he'd probably think I was saying it just because he had. I tugged on his hair as he pulled my body against his.

His hands gripped my hips tightly.

When we finally broke apart we barely separated, just enough to rest our foreheads together while we caught our breath.

"I'm ridiculously in love with you too." The words were out of my mouth before I even realized I'd spoken. So much for not telling him yet.

Dom let out a relieved sigh as the tension left his body,

pressing a kiss to my forehead and sliding his hand into mine as he stepped towards the house. "Come on, let's go in."

"Wait!" I planted my feet to stop us moving as I tugged at his hand. Once he'd turned to face me, I spoke. "Why have you been avoiding being alone with me?"

"It's stupid, but I didn't want you to feel embarrassed about my family hearing us. I know Kat said something to you last time, and I just thought it would be better for you if I didn't put you in that position again." He gave me a sheepish smile.

Going on my tiptoes, I pressed a kiss to his lips. "As much as I appreciate the thought, don't do that again. I thought you had regrets or worse…that I was terrible."

Dom tugged my body against his once more, this time pressing his groin against my stomach. "I only have to think about what we did and I'm rock hard. I don't regret a second of it."

I closed my eyes and let out a groan as heat washed through me at the feel of his hard length.

I wanted him…badly.

"Please tell me that means we're going to bed right now." I begged.

Disappointment filled me as I felt him move away and I opened my eyes to find him looking down at me, a wide grin on his face.

"You bet it fucking does." He gave me a wink before pulling me towards the house.

We didn't see anyone on our way to the bedroom and, to be honest, that was the best outcome. It would have been torture if we'd had to go back into the lounge and slowly figure a way to escape.

I couldn't bear to not touch him after those declarations.

I wanted to brand him as *mine*, and to do that I needed to touch *every* inch of him.

CHAPTER SEVENTEEN

DOM

I KICKED the door shut as soon as Aimee was clear, tugging her against me with the hand I was still holding and running my other hand up her side. Lifting her shirt as I made my way up.

I needed to get her naked. *Now.*

With every inch of skin I uncovered, I realized I'd been an idiot denying myself her beautiful body. I threw her shirt to the floor knowing I was now going to rectify that.

Aimee's hands made quick work of pulling my shirt up, and I lifted my arms allowing her to remove it completely. Her hand trailed over the tattoos on my ribs, all lyrics from my songs.

"Some of these are from the songs you sang tonight." She lifted her eyes to mine. "Country really is in your heart."

I felt my lips turn up in a smile at the thought. "It'll always be country for me."

Surprising me, she pressed a kiss to my pec before teasing my nipple with her tongue. My nipples pebbled, and I bit my lip to help me hold back a moan. My dick hardened within the confines of my jeans, and as she kissed her way down my abdomen I was filled with desperation for some friction.

Aimee's hands moved from my hips to the button on my jeans and I held my breath as she opened them up and moved them downwards with shaky fingers.

"Aim—" I cut my sentence off as I felt her breath against the skin of my cock when it sprang free from my boxers. She'd tugged them down along with my jeans.

I watched her lips part as she stared at my length, and held my breath wondering where she was thinking about taking this. When her tongue poked out and teased the tip, I threw my head back on a groan.

Aimee let out a chuckle before wrapping her luscious lips around my erection, and it sunk into the warmth of her mouth.

"*Jesus…*"

She released my dick and looked at me, a mischievous glint in her eyes. "Have you forgotten my name already?"

I groaned in the back of my throat. "Aimee…"

"Ah. There you go." She threw me a wink before licking her way down my length, clearly loving the power she was holding.

My balls tightened and, when her hand moved to fondle them, I stepped back, making her release my cock with a pop.

"Did I…" The worried look she gave me instantly clued me in on what the rest of her sentence would have been if she hadn't left it hanging.

"No, Aims. I was gonna come."

She grinned. "That's exactly what I was aiming for." Propelling herself forward she sucked me back into her mouth before I could argue. A twirl of her tongue had my eyes closing and all thoughts of pulling away went out of my head. I suddenly needed to come, and couldn't even remember why I'd been holding back before.

"I'm coming." I warned, in case she didn't want me to do it in her mouth, but she didn't move. No, instead she sucked harder, swallowing down everything I released as my legs wobbled, threatening to give way.

Aimee sat back on her heels and I lifted my feet out of the jeans and boxers that were still puddled around my ankles.

I offered Aimee a hand as she got to her feet. "That was…" I shook my head, unable to put it into words, as I pulled her into my arms and crushed my mouth against hers, tasting the salty tang of myself on her tongue.

I backed her towards the bed, needing to return the favor and make her quiver beneath my mouth.

She broke the kiss as the back of her knees hit the edge of the mattress. "Have you decided what that was yet?" she asked, a cheeky grin gracing her face.

"Lay down and I'll show you exactly what that was." It sounded like a dare, and Aimee climbed up the bed slowly, teasingly.

Once she laid her head on the pillow, I climbed up, kneeling between her legs, and unbuttoned her denim shorts excruciatingly slowly. I'd thought it would be torturous for her but I was starting to think it was probably worse for me.

Aimee lifted her ass as I pulled them down her legs. After throwing them to the floor I leant over her body and placed a kiss on her lips. Taking my time, teasing her tongue at a languid pace.

Her hands slid down my sides and zeroed in on my hardening dick.

I pulled back, breaking the kiss and the contact of her fist around my erection. "Ah-ah. You've had your turn."

Grabbing her hands, I held them above her head as I kissed my way down her jaw, her neck. I licked along the lacy edge of her bra's cup before gently biting her nipple through the lace. I could feel it harden beneath my mouth, so I sucked on it too.

Aimee moaned and I lifted my eyes to see her head thrown back, eyes closed, as she enjoyed the sensation. "The heat of your breath mixed with the rough texture of the lace… Dom…" My name was barely a whisper but I wanted to hear her say it just like that, again and again.

My dick was rock hard, you'd never know I'd already gotten off. She turned me on so goddamn much.

"Dom. I need." She called out incoherently, but I knew what she meant and I told her as much.

"I know, baby. I'm going to give you exactly what you need."

I moved down her body, placing kisses here and there as I went.

Her belly button.

Her hipbones.

Her thighs.

Aimee's breath hitched when my lips pressed against her clit and I flicked my tongue out, enjoying the whimpering sounds she was making. She was so needy.

Needy for me.

I let my tongue venture lower and teased her opening. She was wet, warm and ready. Her taste was sweet and in that moment I knew I'd never get enough of her. I slipped in a finger to give her the friction she clearly needed.

"More…" Aimee breathed the word as she rolled her hips.

I slipped in another digit, hooking them slightly as I felt for that magic G-spot, all the while teasing her clit with my tongue. I couldn't take my eyes off her face as she enjoyed the moment.

Aimee lifted her hand to her mouth and bit the flesh on the base of her thumb as she let out another more muffled moan. Her body quivered beneath me and I felt her walls pulse around my fingers.

Removing them, I moved back up her body, reaching for a condom out of the drawers beside the bed. I tore the packet open with my teeth and suited up, all the while watching Aimee come back to earth from her release.

Aimee's eyes popped open and connected with mine as I brushed the tip of my cock against her entrance.

"Please," she begged.

I couldn't do anything but give her what she wanted, not when she pleaded with me like that. I slid my length in to her warmth, inch by slow inch.

Wrapping her legs around my waist she pushed her heels against my ass, forcing me to slam the rest of the way, in to the hilt, eliciting a grunt from my lips. Obviously I wasn't going quickly enough for her.

The head of the bed crashed against the wall and we both froze, looking at each other wide-eyed.

Aimee patted my chest. "Roll over."

I frowned but did as she said, rolling so that our positions were reversed. She'd kept a tight enough grip with her legs that we'd managed to stay connected and I was grateful for that.

Aimee unhooked her legs so I could lie flat on my back, while she knelt over me. She circled her hips and my eyes almost rolled into the back of my head in ecstasy.

"Fuck!"

"That's what I'm doing, Dom." The amusement in her voice had me smiling.

God, I loved this woman. I couldn't help but wonder what I'd done to deserve her.

Gripping Aimee's hips tightly, I guided her up and down, trying to change her pace. Suddenly needing to go fast and hard.

"Yes." Aimee said, leaning her upper body forward and crushing her lips against mine at the same time as she moved on my dick at the perfect pace.

The room filled with muffled moans and I didn't know whether they were mine; hers; or both of ours.

Knowing my orgasm was only seconds away from crashing down on me, I slid my hand away from Aimee's hip and circled my fingers over her clit, needing her to fall with me.

The first squeeze of her walls had my orgasm rolling over me. I felt Aimee, leaning to the side as her body collapsed over mine and I pulled her on top of me, wanting to feel the weight of her body on mine.

Needing to feel her body on mine.

I never wanted to let her go, but my mind kept reminding me that our time together was limited.

Aimee would soon be back in Australia with her family, while I'd have to come home and once again be Saxton.

My heart hurt at the thought.

Because I'd come to the understanding that I'd never be home if I didn't have Aimee in my arms.

CHAPTER EIGHTEEN

AIMEE

YESTERDAY WE'D SPENT the morning back at the hospital. I had test after damn test, but in the end Dr. Petrov gave me the all clear to fly home. We'd once again had a blast on the long ass road trip, playing silly games and sharing stories about our pasts.

Once we'd gotten back to Dom's parents', he'd made some calls and told me he'd managed to get me a flight in two days time. Part of me worried he just wanted to get rid of me, but he had an uncanny way of knowing my thoughts—probably because my face gave them away— and explained that he'd seen me crying every day after talking to my kids, and he knew getting back to them would stop that.

The only thing he didn't realize was that getting back to them meant leaving him, and that would make me just as sad. At least he wouldn't have to witness the crying for that; I was sure I could hide that pain until I was on the plane and out of his sight.

"What's going on in that pretty head of yours?" Dom asked, before pressing a kiss to my temple.

I'd been staring out the bedroom window, watching the

birds fly from tree to tree in Dom's parents' backyard as I waited for him to finish in the bathroom.

I turned to face him and gave him a smile that I hoped didn't look as fake as it felt. "Nothing much, just wondering what movies will be on the flight."

Dom gave me a knowing look but didn't question me further. Instead, he pressed a quick kiss to my lips before striding to the closet. "I'm going to have to pick my shirt wisely, you look gorgeous."

My face blushed at his words but he didn't witness it since he was pulling his choice of shirt over his head. I turned back to the window. "Thanks. It's just an old dress."

Dom's hands gripped my biceps and he turned me to face him. "Well, you make this old dress look good."

I took in his purple shirt and ran my hands up over the buttons, straightening the collar. "You look pretty handsome yourself."

Reaching onto my tiptoes I pressed a gentle kiss to Dom's lips, taking it further when he opened to me. My hands slid around his neck and I had to force myself not to muss his hair as they itched to sink into the dark strands.

A knock sounded on the door and we parted lips, but didn't step apart. "Dom, Aimee. Are you two ready?"

"Y—" Dom cleared his throat and tried again. "Yeah, Mom. We'll be down in a second."

"You really don't have to go to all this trouble for me. I'd be more than happy just to eat here and watch some TV," I said, not for the first time that day.

They'd decided we had to go out for a fancy meal to say goodbye. I didn't know what bothered me most, the fact that we were eating at a fancy restaurant when I was anything but fancy, or that it was a 'goodbye' meal and it made me so much more aware of leaving these amazing people the next day? Plus, they'd already made it perfectly clear the meal was on them and I hated not paying for myself.

Dom slipped his hand into mine. "Mom's already made her mind up and there's no changing it, so you just have to go with it. Try to enjoy it." Lifting our joined hands he pressed a kiss to the back of mine before pulling us out the door and downstairs to his family.

———

I STARED WIDE-EYED at the giant ice cream sundae the waiter placed in front of Dom who was sat opposite me. "Are you seriously going to eat *all* of that?"

He didn't answer, just scooped out a spoonful of chocolate syrup covered ice cream and placed it in his mouth.

"He does it every time we come here. It's like a ritual," Kat admitted from beside me.

I turned to look at her. "Even after eating a huge steak?"

"Every damn time," his father confirmed before he placed a spoonful of brownie in his mouth.

I once again gave Kat my attention. "So what are your plans now that you've got some time at home?"

Kat lifted her wine to her lips and had a sip before answering. "Honestly, I haven't really thought about it much. I guess I'll see if Damo needs a hand at the bakery. I love working there."

I glanced at Dom, thinking about asking him the same question, but his attention was so focused on his dessert I didn't think I'd get a reply even if I did ask.

"Aimee, what's the first thing you're going to do once you get home?" Rose asked, giving me her full attention as she rested her chin on her hands.

I frowned. "Apart from kissing my kids and sleeping, I haven't really considered it."

She nodded. "It's hard being away from your kids."

"It is. This was supposed to be a two-week trip, yet it's turned into five weeks. I miss them like crazy." I widened my eyes. "What am I saying? You'll know exactly how hard it is. I bet you're glad you've got your kids back for a while."

Rose's eyes flicked over all three of her kids before she spoke. "Some longer than others." She sighed. I frowned, not following her, but before I could question it she waved off my confusion. "Anyway, let's have a toast." She lifted her glass and held it out.

The rest of us did the same with our own glasses.

"To new friends; to family. May we stay connected for a lifetime."

Tears filled my eyes at her sentiment. I really wanted what she was toasting but deep down I knew we'd lose touch. It was inevitable. Once I got on that plane, Dom would get back to being the famous Saxton and he'd forget all about me.

They all would.

The thought made my heart hurt and I could only imagine how painful it would be once I was in the air.

After we all clinked glasses, I discreetly wiped away my tears and watched Dom as he placed the last spoonful of his sundae in his mouth before slouching back in his chair with a groan, a hand resting over his stomach.

"You didn't have to eat it all." I gave him a raised eyebrow as he sat with his eyes closed, most probably fighting off a sugar coma.

Dom popped open one eye like it was too hard to open them both. "I did. It's bad luck if I don't."

I wanted to laugh but he seemed so serious, I didn't dare, fearful of insulting him.

Luckily, Rose saved me from having to reply. "Why don't you kids go spend a few hours dancing?" Her eyes landed on her husband. "Come on Calvin, let's go home." She stood, giving him no chance for argument.

"Have fun kids," Calvin stated, as he rose from his seat and grabbed Rose's hand. They walked out of the restaurant, pausing at the counter to settle the bill on their way out.

Dom groaned once again. "I won't be able to walk to the car. There's no chance of me dancing."

"My flight's pretty early, right Dom?"

Dom still hadn't told me the full details. When he'd booked it, I'd said I didn't want to know the specifics because I'd be so conflicted with how to feel. I'd want to count down the hours to see my kids but that would also mean wishing away my remaining time with Dom. I felt torn in two and I didn't think that feeling would go away anytime soon.

"It is," Dom answered, not bothering to open his eyes. "What are you thinking…an early night?"

"Yeah, I think that will be best," I said, even though the real reason I wanted to go back to the house was so that I could spend the rest of my time wrapped in his arms. I didn't care about sleeping. I'd get plenty of that on the plane.

"We'll have more fun without you anyway, Bro," Alberto stated, slapping Dom on the shoulder before giving me an apologetic look. "We'll miss you though, Aims."

Kat chuckled. "It's always you that gets recognized, Dom, and makes us leave, so yeah, I have to agree with Al."

Dom rolled his eyes as they headed for the exit. He didn't seem in a hurry to move so I stayed where I was, letting him have whatever time he needed to settle his stomach.

After a couple of minutes he straightened in the chair. "Let's go."

Once outside I started to head for the car park where we'd left the two vehicles we'd come in, but Dom slipped his arm over my shoulder and steered me in the opposite direction. "I want to take you for a stroll first. I think I need to walk that sundae off."

I giggled. "I thought you said you wouldn't even make it to the car?"

"That was just a ploy to get you to myself," he stated, pressing a kiss to the side of my head.

My heart fluttered in my chest at the idea of him wanting to spend this time with just me. Although we'd both declared our love on his verandah the other night—and I had no doubts we meant every word—neither of us had said it again.

We came to a stop in the middle of a darkened park. It was away from the streetlights and when he tugged me down, sitting on the ground and told me to look up, I did.

Lying down on the grass beside him I took in the beautiful sight above us. The night sky was full of twinkling stars with not a cloud in sight to hide them. "Do you know anything about stars?" I asked as the cool, but pleasant, breeze blew a strand of hair across my face. I brushed it away, tucking it behind my ear.

"Not really. It wasn't something I was interested in growing up. You?" His hand slipped into mine, our fingers entwining.

My lips turned up in a smile, enjoying the affection he was showing me. "No. I know the Southern Cross—only because it's on the Australian flag—and that's about it."

Dom laughed but didn't speak anymore and it was nice reclining beside him in the silence as we both stared up at the night sky. It somehow made me feel like I wouldn't be so far away from him once I got back to Australia. All I'd have to do at any given moment was look up at the stars above me and know that he was somewhere under that same sky.

It was a comforting thought and I held on to it, hoping it would get me through some of the sad days I knew I had ahead of me.

CHAPTER NINETEEN

DOM

IT WAS STILL DARK when the alarm went off and I wanted to press snooze and snuggle back under the covers, but we had a flight to catch.

I stroked Aimee's cheek gently in an effort to wake her up. "Baby, you gotta get up."

Aimee groaned and burrowed her head against my chest. "It's too early, even the sun agrees."

"The flight won't wait," I stated as I ran a hand over her hair, loving the feel of the soft silky strands falling through my fingers.

She huffed. "Fine." Aimee lifted her upper body and leant in to press a kiss to my lips, only she paused before our mouths could make contact "I'll get up. But first…" She left her sentence hanging as she closed the distance between our lips before sliding the rest of her body on top of mine and making it perfectly clear what she wanted to do first.

We'd made love last night…more than once.

I could never get enough of her sweet curves so there was no chance of me turning her down this morning, even if we were short on time.

Aimee rubbed her warm, slick core against my dick and I groaned into her mouth. She pushed against my chest, breaking the kiss and lifting herself into a sitting position astride me. Her hands went between us as she raised her hips and gripped my dick, giving it a sure stroke before guiding it to her entrance.

Her bouncing tits caught my attention and my hands slid up from her hips to cup them. Rolling her nipples between my thumb and forefinger enticed a moan from her lips as she threw her head back, not slowing her pace.

"You're so fucking beautiful."

Leaning forward, Aimee crushed her lips against mine.

I slipped my hands down to her ass, gripping it tightly as she moved on my dick at the perfect pace. My balls tightened and my spine tingled as her walls started to pulse.

"Dom!" she cried out as she came, her pace becoming erratic as she lost herself in her orgasm and triggered my own release.

Aimee relaxed on top of me and I stroked a hand over her back as we both recovered, our heaving breathing filling the room. She squirmed and my dick slipped free, and it was in that moment as the air hit my wet dick that I realized our mistake.

We hadn't used a condom.

"Shit!"

"I'm sorry."

We both spoke at the same time.

Aimee's apology caught my attention as she buried her face in my chest. "I can't believe I was so stupid."

"It takes two. This doesn't just fall on you," I stated. Seeing no reaction to my words I needed to know she was listening to me. "Look at me, Aims."

Following my command Aimee lifted her head and her eyes, brimming with concern, connected with mine.

"I'm with you in this, okay?" She nodded at my words and I pressed a kiss to her forehead. "Let's not worry prematurely."

"Okay." She gave me a brief smile. "It took me a year of trying to fall pregnant with Dan anyway, and I'm almost ten years older and much less fertile now."

"Come on, we've got to get going," I said after placing one last peck on her lips.

We both shifted off the bed, Aimee pulling on one of my shirts as I grabbed a pair of boxers. It had become our morning routine.

"Am I okay getting a quick shower, or will I wake everyone up?" Aimee asked, grabbing her change of clothes and doing everything to avoid my eyes.

I pulled her back against my chest and placed a kiss on the curve of her neck, feeling the tension leave her as she relaxed into my hold. "Everyone will already be awake. They won't let you leave without saying goodbye."

Aimee bent her neck giving me more room to place my kisses. "Oh, well, I wanted to say goodbye to them too. It's just early and I didn't expect..." she explained, trailing off, clearly distracted by the butterfly kisses I was placing on her skin. Her breathing became heavier.

A knock sounded on the door. "Are you two awake?" Mom's voice called through the wood.

I released Aimee and pulled open the door. "Yeah, we're up. Aimee was just heading for the bathroom."

Aimee offered my mom a quick smile as she made her way to the shower.

"I'm going to go and make you both a bacon sandwich." The bathroom door clicked shut and Mom's voice dropped to a whisper. "We can't have you both flying on an empty stomach."

"Thanks, Mom," I said as I gave her a brief hug. Her

words reminded me I still had a secret I was keeping from Aimee, and in order to keep it for a little longer I had to get my suitcase downstairs and in the truck before she finished in the bathroom.

Mom headed for the kitchen and I turned back to my room, throwing on the first clothes I came across. I quickly pulled out my packed suitcase, which I'd hid in the back of the closet, and headed downstairs with it.

Al met me by the front door. "I'll take that, you go get Aimee's so she doesn't see yours when we put it in the trunk."

That was a good idea; I'd not even considered that possibility. I ran back upstairs and grabbed not only Aimee's case but my backpack, too, knowing that would need to be kept out of sight as well.

After locking it all in the trunk, I walked back into the house, not at all surprised when I found Aimee at the top of the stairs. She'd never seemed to take long in the bathroom, not like my sister did. God, Kat would spend hours in the shower if the hot water didn't run out, and her hair was nowhere near as long as Aimee's.

"I was just putting your suitcase in the car."

Sliding her hands around my neck, she reached up, taking my mouth with hers in a slow savoring kiss. I could taste the fresh, minty toothpaste on her tongue as it brushed up against mine.

It wasn't long before Aimee broke the kiss, pulling back just enough to look me in the eyes. "I'm gonna miss this."

I bit my lip, wondering whether to tell her she didn't have to worry about that yet, but decided to stick with the plan and tell her at the airport. I just hoped to hell she wouldn't end up upset over the fact that I was actually going with her. *That would be pretty embarrassing.*

"Mom is making breakfast. I'm just going to get showered

and changed. Okay?" I said, trying to change the subject without spoiling my surprise.

I really did hope that she'd be happy when she found out I'd be going with her; that we'd get to spend more time together.

I wanted to try and make this thing between us work, even though I knew it would be hard and we'd have long periods of separation. I felt like we'd be able handle it.

The feelings I had for her were something I'd never had for anyone else and I just knew we could go for the long haul, no matter how rough a road we chose to take.

CHAPTER TWENTY

AIMEE

WITH EACH MINUTE THAT PASSED, each kilometer closer to the airport we got, my heart started to hurt more and more. I knew I was getting closer to walking out of Dom's life for good.

A man I'd come to love.

A man I'd fallen head over heels for.

And I hated it.

Dom's hand squeezed mine and I glanced at him beside me, giving him a small smile that I knew didn't reach my eyes, but it was the best I could offer under the circumstances. Dom didn't seem upset about me leaving, that we'd probably never see each other again—and that hurt like hell—but it made me at least try to hide my own pain.

"You two have been pretty quiet," Rose pointed out from the front seat. The whole Saxton family wanted to wave me off, which was a nice gesture. Rose and Calvin offered to drive us, while Alberto and Kat followed behind in another vehicle.

Calvin suddenly turned off the main road and my heart started hammering in my chest as my stomach churned with nerves. I wasn't the most comfortable of flyers. As a kid, I'd been a really bad traveller, suffering sickness whenever I went anywhere, no matter what transport I took. As I grew older I learned how to manage it, but flying was still my nemesis. Especially if I let the nerves get the better of me.

In no time at all, we were exiting the vehicles and Dom was opening up the trunk.

I glanced at the contents and frowned in confusion at what I saw. Not only was my suitcase in there, but there was a second one and a backpack too.

I glanced at Dom, my eyebrows still drawn, and held my arm up to shade my eyes from the rising sun behind him. "Is someone else going somewhere too?"

Dom gave me a sheepish look as he shrugged. "Well, I guess that depends on you. I booked myself a ticket as well. Is it okay if I come and spend some time with you in Australia?"

My jaw almost hit the floor as tears welled in my eyes.

"Look, it's fine. I don't have—"

"Okay? Did you just ask if it was okay? That is the best news. Ever!" I admitted, cutting him off as I lunged at him, throwing my arms around his neck. When he lifted me up I wrapped my legs around his waist and pressed a kiss to his mouth, tasting the salt from my tears as they rolled freely down my cheeks. I couldn't even begin to process how I felt. Dom was coming with me, which meant I didn't have to say goodbye to him any time soon.

Dom pulled back from the kiss and placed me on my feet. Cupping my face, he wiped at my tears with his thumbs. "If it's the best news ever why are you crying?" He affectionately pressed a kiss to the tip of my nose.

"They're happy tears…I promise." Turning my head, I pressed a kiss to the palm of his hand. "Unbelievable, ecstatic, happy tears."

"Well if that's the case, we've got a flight to catch!" Dom

stated, excitement clear in his voice. He wrapped his arm around my waist and pulled me into his side, turning us to face the others.

I spotted our suitcases, which were now out of the trunk and on the ground beside us. Alberto or Calvin having probably pulled them out during our distraction.

"We..." I said in disbelief as a wide smile spread across my face—a smile I didn't think would be going anywhere anytime soon.

Dom just made my day.

Hell, maybe even my year.

"That we do." My heart soared with as the words left my mouth.

———

DOM HAD BOOKED us first class tickets, which meant we'd had access to the first-class lounge and we were allowed to board first, avoiding the majority of the crowds.

Spending the long flight in those big seats that let you recline all the way back was amazing. Being comfortable really helped with the travel sickness too. I was pretty sure first class had ruined me for all my future travel plans but it was an experience I wouldn't want to change for the world.

Dom pulled on a hoodie and tugged a cap over his head as we landed to help disguise him while we walked through the airport. As far as we knew people still thought he was in the US, but we'd been in the air for hours and you never knew what stories may have broken in that length of time.

I glanced at Dom in his thick hoodie as we walked behind a guy in a suit pulling along his shiny black suitcase, and couldn't help but feel bad for him. It may be autumn in Queensland, but it would still be pretty humid meaning the minute he walked outside he was going to be pretty damn uncomfortable. Thankfully, in the car he'd be able to take it off. Or at least I hoped that was his plan because I was feeling uncomfortable just looking at the hoodie and we hadn't even stepped out of the airport's air-conditioning yet.

As we stepped through the glass doors to the arrivals waiting area, my eyes flitted through the crowd, having no idea who would be here to greet us. I'd originally driven Sam and me here when we'd left, but she'd taken my keys with her while I was in a coma. After all, she'd needed a way for her and Matt to get home.

Dom had secretly sent everyone our flight details before we left—which he'd fessed up about during the flight—so I knew someone had to be here to pick us up.

A body barreled into me and I stumbled back at the impact as the person's arms wrapped around me. Dom's hand pressed against my back, steadying me. I looked down at the top of a dark head of hair and instantly knew it was my youngest son, Dan.

"I missed you so much." His voice was so full of emotion that I wasn't surprised to see tear filled eyes when he lifted his head and locked them with mine.

I had to fight my own emotions as I took in the sight of him. Well, what little I could see as he squeezed me tight. "I missed you too, buddy."

"Hey, stop hogging her. We all want hugs," Chris, my oldest, complained.

My eyes fell on him, and nearly popped out of my head as Dan stepped back, releasing me. As Chris stopped in front of me, I discovered he'd most definitely had a growth spurt during the time I'd been in the US. He was almost a whole head higher than me.

"Jesus, you've grown. What the hell have you been eating?" I questioned, looking up at him in wonder.

"Everything. He doesn't stop," My mum answered and I

looked around Chris to see everyone here. Mum, Dad, Reece, Sam, and even Matt.

Matt pulled Dom into a manly hug and they patted each other's backs as everyone stepped up to me, giving me hug after hug.

I turned to introduce Dom to everyone but noticed a few people looking our way and decided it was time to go. We were drawing attention and I didn't want to ruin Dom's chances at anonymity. "Maybe we should head to the car?" I suggested.

Everyone nodded their agreement, most likely noticing the same things I had.

My dad tugged my suitcase out of my hold, and took my mum's hand in his other hand, before leading the way out of the airport.

Once we reached the cars—my dad's and mine parked side by side—Sam held out my keys. "Do you want to drive?"

Sam wasn't the biggest fan of driving, especially since we drove on the opposite side of the road to what she was used to in her home country of Germany. I took the keys out of her hand with a smile. She'd only been living here for the last couple of months and I kept telling her she just hadn't had enough practice to feel comfortable, but she always shrugged it of and insisted practice wouldn't make a difference. She just didn't like being behind the wheel.

My dad lifted my suitcase into the boot of his car as the kids one by one gave me another hug, before sliding into the back of it.

"Dad, this is Dom. Dom, this is my dad, Spencer," I introduced the two as we stood at the back of the cars, suddenly feeling bad that I hadn't done it back at the arrivals lounge.

Dad reached out and shook Dom's hand. "Nice to meet you, Dom."

"You too, Spencer," Dom greeted.

"Thanks for looking after our baby girl," Mum said stepping up beside me.

Letting go of his suitcase, Dom opened his arms and she stepped straight into them. "It's nice to finally meet you, Sarah."

Dom's words reminded me that while I'd been in a coma at the hospital they'd been Face Timing on a daily basis. It was weird to think about but they had a connection before Dom and I did.

"You're even more handsome in the flesh." As Mum pulled away, the embarrassment of her words was obvious in the blush coloring her cheeks.

I had to duck my head to hide my grin. It was good seeing someone else affected by Dom the same way I was.

I'd missed my family fiercely these last few weeks and it was so nice to finally be back with them, but what made it even more amazing was the fact my loved ones would get the chance to know the guy who'd stolen my heart.

CHAPTER TWENTY-ONE

DOM

I SAT on the couch watching Aimee with her kids. They were talking over each other while filling her in on all the things she'd missed over the last few weeks, and I was amazed how she seemed to be following all three kids and their stories without missing a beat. And stories were exactly what her youngest, Dan, was telling her. Unless there'd been real sightings of dragons and griffins that I'd somehow missed on the news.

Aimee's eyes caught mine and she offered me a small smile before focusing back on her kids.

"Do you want one?" Spencer offered, holding a bottle of beer up in the kitchen.

The kitchen, dining and lounge where all one open plan room in the shape of an L, which made it surprisingly homely since you could interact as a family no matter which area you were in.

"Thanks," I said gratefully, taking the cold bottle as he handed it over.

"Mummy, can we watch the newest Avengers movie? You

still haven't seen it yet. Please?" Dan begged, holding his hands together in prayer and dropping onto his knees.

"There's some popcorn in the cupboard and there might even be some lollies too," Sarah interjected, pointing over her shoulder in the direction of the kitchen.

Aimee's smile widened. "A family movie night sounds like a great idea. Why don't we get all the quilts and pillows off the beds so we can get comfortable on the floor since it'll be a tight fit on the sofa?"

The kids all jumped up and rushed off to their rooms as Aimee stood.

"I'll go get the popcorn ready," Sarah announced before dashing off.

Sam slid forward off the couch where she'd been sitting with Matt. "Aims do you want to sit here? I'm happy to sit on the floor."

"No, stay there. I'm going to go get my quilt and pillows to make a comfortable spot right here." Aimee pointed to the floor at her feet. "I'll have the perfect view." She headed towards her room and I followed, pausing in the doorway to lean against the frame.

"Do you need a hand?"

Aimee jumped, spinning around with a hand clutched against her chest. "Jesus, you scared me."

Pushing off the doorframe, I took a few short steps and stopped in front of her. I brushed a strand of hair behind her ear.

"Hey," she said as she gave me a sweet smile. Her hands slid around my waist pulling us closer together.

"Hey." I pressed my lips lightly against hers in a butterfly kiss.

"I'm sorry we haven't had much alone time since arriving."

I pressed another kiss to her lips. "Shh. Don't apologize.

Your family needs this time with you. They've been worried about you."

"Muuum. We're all ready and waiting on you and Dom," Reece shouted, the break in his voice mid-sentence being the only reason that I knew it was him and not his older brother. I'd noticed throughout the day that his voice tended to break quite often when he was speaking.

"On our way," she called over my shoulder before stealing a quick kiss and releasing me to step back towards the bed. "I'll get the quilt, can you grab the pillows?"

"Sure thing." I did as she asked and followed her back into the lounge. The spot Aimee had pointed out to Sam was the only empty place between the couch and the TV. The kids had taken up the rest.

Sam, Matt, Sarah and Spencer were all spread out on the long L shaped couch.

I stood with the pillows as Aimee made quick work of getting the quilt exactly how she wanted it, making me think she'd done this before, and on more than one occasion.

"Okay. Pillows need to go there and there," she ordered, pointing to exactly where she wanted them. "Perfect." She sat down and patted the spot beside her, inviting me to do the same.

It didn't take me long to take up the invitation and the second she cuddled into my side, I was so grateful to Dan for suggesting the movie night in the first place I decided then and there I needed to buy the kid chocolate or something.

This moment was perfect—Aimee pressed against me and her family surrounding her.

———

THE MOVIE ENDED and the sound of bodies stretching filled the air. Halfway through the movie Dan had curled into

Aimee's side and proceeded to snore within seconds. He'd barely let her out of his sight since we arrived which made it clear he was happy to have her back.

"Come on, chicken, it's time for bed." Aimee nudged Dan's side. His eyes popped open but they were glassy and unfocused. She guided him to stand, her hands under his arms, and he complied without question or complaint. "Dom, do you mind bringing his stuff?"

"On it," I stated, having already reached for his pillow as they both stood. Grabbing the things, I walked behind them as they slowly made their way to his room. Leaving Aimee to tuck him in, I headed back to the lounge.

Chris and Reece were nowhere to be seen, along with their things, and I could only assume they'd already left to get ready for bed.

Aimee walked back through the room and, rather than coming back to the lounge, she headed off in the other direction. I guessed she was going to say goodnight to her two other sons.

I sat back on our pile of covers and watched the episode of Mrs. Brown's Boys that the others were watching. After a few minutes Aimee returned, sitting back down beside me once again and I relaxed as she settled into the crook of my arm.

Once the episode ended Sarah stood, stretching noisily. "Come on Spencer, let's go to bed. Goodnight everyone."

Aimee's breathing had evened out about five minutes into the show, so I wasn't surprised when she didn't react to her mum's bid goodnight.

Sarah glanced from Aimee to me. "Make sure she gets to bed?" It sounded like a question so I nodded.

"Yes, Ma'am."

She giggled and elbowed Spencer's side. "Did you hear that? He called me Ma'am."

Spencer threw his arm around his wife's shoulder and pulled her away with a shake of his head. "Come on, Darls. Bed's calling, remember?" He gave us a wave over his shoulder as they made their way to their bedroom.

Sam stretched and Matt helped her up off the couch. "I guess we should call it night too, otherwise I'll end up carrying you to bed."

"You love carrying me to bed." She poked out her tongue and I couldn't help but smile at how their relationship had grown since they'd left America. Matt was my childhood best friend. Hell, he was like another brother and it was so good to see him happy with someone.

Matt laughed. "It is becoming somewhat of a habit. Three times this week already and we're only on Thursday."

Sam shrugged as she walked backwards out of the room. "I don't know what you're complaining about, it sounds like the habit's broken to me." She turned and headed to what I could only assume to be her room. "Night Dom," she called over her shoulder.

"Night Sam." I focused my attention on Matt, his hair was freshly ruffled, making me think he must have run his hand through it while I was watching Sam. "You two seem to be going well."

The smile that graced his face lit him up. "We are. It's crazy to think how fast things are moving but…I'm happy. And it feels right." His eyes dropped to Aimee curled on the floor at our feet. "I guess you understand what I mean."

"I think I do." I smiled. We had a man hug and I wished him goodnight.

"I hope you manage to sleep through. The jet lag just about drove me crazy," he stated before heading in the same direction that Sam had disappeared.

Crouching down I gently nudged Aimee awake. "Aims, are we going to go to bed?"

"Hmmm. Dom?" she mumbled, but didn't move.

I stroked a finger over her cheek, causing her to swipe at my hand as if it was a stray insect. "Aimee…everyone's gone to bed." Deciding it was no use. I scooped her up into my arms.

The movement caused her to finally stir. Her tired eyes locking with mine, confusion written in the crease of her brow.

"Hey there, Sleeping Beauty." I placed a kiss on her cute scrunched up brow.

"Did I fall asleep?" She rested her head against my shoulder as I walked us into her bedroom.

"You did," I admitted as I placed her down on her side of the bed, thinking how funny it was that we had sides and how easily we'd manage to just slip into a routine with each other. "I'll be back, I'm just going to go get the pillows and stuff." I turned on the lamp on her bedside table before stepping away.

Making sure the TV was turned off, I grabbed the quilt and pillows and flicked off the light switch on the way out of the room, following the warm glow of the lamp back to Aimee's room.

When I made it back to the bedroom, Aimee was wearing some sleeping shorts and a tank top.

A tank top with my face on it.

I burst out laughing as I threw the covers on the bed.

"What?" Aimee asked, feigning innocence.

I gave her a questioning look as my eyes dropped to my face plastered tightly across her ample chest.

She looked down. "Oh, this? It's my favorite tank. I can only wear it to bed because, as you can see, I bought the wrong size."

Shaking my head I pulled her into my arms. "It's a good job you're cute, otherwise I might worry you're a stalker or something." I pressed a kiss to the tip of her nose as she looked up at me.

"Hey, you're the one that had a charity campaign that gave me the opportunity to sleep with you before I even met you."

I laughed at her logic. "Well, I guess you have a point. Get in bed before I strip you of the top altogether." I tapped her butt playfully, making my own point.

Aimee made a show of thinking, placing her finger against her cheek. "I can't decide which would be the better outcome?" She gave me a cheeky grin before slipping into the bed and under the covers.

After dropping my shorts and pulling off my shirt, I slipped into the bed wearing just my boxers.

Aimee instantly wrapped herself around me as I settled down on the pillow, making me grin. I loved how cuddly she was with me. I'd heard people talk about that kind of thing, calling it clingy and needy, but god…I wouldn't have it any other way.

I'd come to love this woman so deeply; I didn't think I'd be able to survive without her in my life.

And I knew for a fact I wouldn't want to.

CHAPTER TWENTY-TWO

AIMEE

I OPENED my eyes in the dark room with my mind wide-awake, causing me to curse myself for falling asleep in front of the TV. I knew before reaching for my phone that it had to be stupid o'clock in the morning.

Yep. Four o'clock to be precise.

I groaned quietly, hoping not to wake Dom up. If he could manage to sleep through without jet lag being a bitch then I wasn't going to ruin that for him.

Slowly and gently, I slipped out from under his arm and smiled as he snuggled further beneath the sheet. I still couldn't believe he was here with me. Never in my wildest dreams had I imagined him booking himself a ticket. I'd been so stuck on leaving him and never seeing him again I hadn't been able to see any other outcome.

Grabbing my backpack I headed into the lounge. I didn't bother turning on any lights because I didn't want to wake anyone else up and I knew my MacBook would give me enough light to type. I'd started a story at Dom's parents' and the characters didn't seem to want to shut up, so I thought making the most out of the crappy jet lag was as good a plan as any.

"Hey," Dom's sleepy voice spoke quietly behind me, pulling my attention away from the story that'd had me clicking away at the keyboard.

I turned to watch him walk around the sofa before glancing at the time on my MacBook. I'd only been writing for fifteen minutes. "I thought I'd managed to slip out without waking you. I'm sorry."

Dom rubbed a hand over his face as he sat beside me. "You didn't wake me, my brain did. It's clearly on US time even though my eyes and body aren't." He glanced at the screen on my lap and gave me a wide smile. "You're writing again."

I grinned, I may have only been writing for fifteen minutes but the words were flowing thick and fast which was not the norm for me. Although, if you asked my best friend, Samantha, she'd say it was because I'd grown so much as an author in the last year.

Writing daily was the key and I would have never found that without her.

"I am," I confirmed.

"Do you mind if I grab my notebook and join you? I've had some lyrics playing over in my head for the last couple of days, I guess it's about time I put pen to paper."

"I'd love the company," I admitted truthfully. I'd be happy spending every minute of the rest of my life with him.

Only, that wasn't realistic so for the time being I'd take whatever I could.

"Great." He pressed a kiss to my temple before getting up and heading for the bedroom where his notebook was.

We both wrote for the next couple of hours, just the scratch of his pencil on the paper and the tapping of my keys filling the silence of the room as the light from the rising sun started to slowly seep in.

A door opened and I turned to spot my Dad walking into the kitchen.

"Morning. Have you two been up long?" he asked as he made quick work of his usual morning routine.

Closing my MacBook, I placed it on the seat next to me and gave Dom's knee a gentle squeeze as I stood and stretched before joining my dad in the kitchen.

I glanced at the clock on the microwave. "A couple of hours. We'll probably need a nap later."

Dad nodded as he pulled together his sandwich for lunch. "Not too late, or you'll be doing it all again tomorrow."

I laughed. "Pfft…I have a feeling I'll be doing it again tomorrow, nap or no nap."

Before Sam arrived here, I'd gone to Germany to spend some time with her and her family while my kids were at their dad's for the school holidays. She'd come back with me and we'd suffered for weeks, waking up at stupid times of the night and not being able to get back to sleep. We'd then find ourselves in desperate need of a nap in the middle of the day. We tried no naps. Early nights. You name it. Nothing worked. I'd thought I'd never sleep through the night again, but thankfully, *eventually* it just happened. Now, with my recent travels, I'd gone and messed that up again.

I grabbed a couple of cups off the rack, deciding a coffee would probably do me and Dom good since the kids would be getting up soon. They weren't going to school today because they'd managed to talk me into letting them have the day off. They insisted we needed to take Dom and Matt to the Australia Zoo. The zoo that Steve Irwin, 'The Crocodile Hunter', had made famous. I'm such a softy. It's Friday and Saturday, a non-school day, is one day away and I still said yes.

"Ooh, can I have one of those?" My mum asked from behind me as she gave me a quick hug over my shoulder, trying not to disturb my coffee making.

"Did you smell the coffee or something?" I asked shaking my head at her uncanny timing.

She laughed. "Nope. I've just got impeccable timing."

I rolled my eyes and slid a cup towards her. "Enjoy!" Grabbing the other two cups, I followed behind my mum as she headed for the lounge.

"Morning Dom."

He lifted his head sharply, as if her words had brought him back to the moment rather than wherever his muse had taken him as he was scribbling down his lyrics. "Sarah, hi." He flicked his eyes to mine and I offered him a cup.

"Coffee?"

Dom took it quickly, his shoulders slumping in relief as he had a sip. "Oh, I love you. Thank you."

I saw Mum's eyes widen in surprise out of the corner of mine before she caught herself and smiled.

"Well, if you only love me for the coffee…" I reached for the cup, pretending to take it away.

Dom pulled it back out of my reach. "I love you regardless of the coffee. Please, don't take it away from me." The fake terror in his voice had both Mum and me laughing.

"Oh damn…I missed the coffee," Sam complained from the kitchen.

"Looks like you'll just have to make your own, Sammy," I called over my shoulder.

"Ha! You're forgetting I have this wonderful man who just loves to make coffee for me. Isn't that right, Matt?"

Looking over my shoulder I watched as Matt pulled her against him, his hands on her hips. He placed a fierce kiss on her lips before leaning back just a fraction, to look her in the eyes. "Anything for my sweetheart."

After another forceful kiss, Sam stepped back and leaned against the wall as she watched him making the coffee in just a pair of shorts.

It was nice to see Sam so in love and receiving the love back in return. She'd been without someone for a long time and if anyone deserved the head-over-heels-reciprocated-love I could see happening in that kitchen, it was Sam.

"They're cute together."

Dom's words drew my attention back to the lounge and I turned around settling back into my seat.

Dom wrapped his arm around my shoulder and I snuggled into his side.

"They aren't the only ones," Mum muttered half under her breath.

Dad took a seat beside her his cup of tea held steady in one hand. "I know, they're almost as cute as us," he said as he placed his other arm over her shoulders and tugged her against his side before planting a sloppy kiss on her cheek.

"Ugh, Pop. My eyes!" Chris complained as he came into the room. "I'll be scarred for life. Reece, save yourself, don't come out here."

Dom slipped his hand in mine and I watched as his thumb brushed over my knuckles. He caught me watching and lifted our hands, placing a kiss on the back of mine with a smile.

"Are we really having the day off school?" Reece asked, an apprehensive look on his face as he rounded the couch. "You never let us have a day off. Unless we're, like, really sick."

I shrugged. "You can go to school if you really want to—"

An echo of three resounding 'NOs' cut my sentence short as Dan joined us.

"Well, in that case, you best all get some cereal because we want to get to the zoo early." The words had barely left my mouth before all three kids practically ran for the kitchen.

"Hey…Careful! I nearly spilt my elixir of life, I haven't even had a sip," Sam complained her voice getting closer with every word, telling me she was heading this way.

Dad sighed and stood. "Well, some of us actually have to go to work. I'll see you all tonight." He pressed a quick kiss to my mum's cheek before straightening again. "I would tell you all to have a good day but I don't want you to." He stuck out his tongue playfully and I rolled my eyes.

My parents could be worse than the kids sometimes, but I wouldn't swap them for the world.

In fact, being away from them had only confirmed that bringing the kids to live with my parents after my separation was the best thing for us. We were the happiest we'd been as a family in a long time. Well, when you didn't count the days my ex's interfering fiancé overstepped her boundaries. She was more than welcome to my ex, but she was not welcome to start acting like my kids' mother. They already had one of those.

My life—and her life—would be much less stressful if she'd just understand that.

CHAPTER TWENTY-THREE

DOM

WALKING hand in hand with Aimee through the zoo and watching her kids' bright smiles as we saw the different exhibits while the sun beat down on us made for a perfect day. I was surprised at how polite and well-behaved Aimee's kids were. Don't get me wrong, they'd have their fights and some back-chatting moments like all children did, but overall they were good kids.

The fact that they seemed to be dealing with their parents' separation pretty well made me wonder what Aimee and her ex's relationship might have been like beforehand. Could it have been volatile? She'd told me they'd been together since they were teenagers and had grown apart—that they'd wanted different things, but I had a feeling that wasn't the whole story. Not that it was any of my business; I just wanted to be there for her if she needed a shoulder.

"Mummy, come look at this…quick," Dan said, grabbing Aimee's free hand and trying to tug her towards the next exhibit.

I released her other hand so I wasn't slowing them down. "Go."

Hearing my words made Dan turn. "No, you've got to come too, Dom."

I smiled at his command and, grabbing Aimee's hand again, we all ran, joining Chris and Reece who stood at a railing overlooking a large crocodile enclosure.

There was a guy standing on a raised platform over the water. He reached into a bucket, pulled out what looked like a dead chicken and placed it on the end of a stick he held it out over the water. Within seconds the biggest crocodile I'd ever seen leapt out of the water and took the chicken right off the stick.

"Holy fuck!"

A few nearby parents glared at me and I gave them an apologetic look for my swearing in front of their kids. I was usually good about not swearing around children but damn, if you saw this croc you'd probably swear too.

My eyes fell on Aimee who was suppressing a laugh by biting at her lip. I stepped in close behind her, effectively caging her against the railing, before whispering in her ear. "If you don't stop biting that lip, I'll give them more than just a swear word to glare at me for."

Aimee turned her head just enough so that I'd be able to hear her own whispered words. "Is that a promise?"

"You are a naughty girl, Miss Jonas." I shook my head as I tried to remind myself that we were in public and all the things I wanted to do to her were frowned upon with audiences.

"You two can kiss in front of us, you know?" Reece stated. "You've seen what we have to witness between Nan and Pop." He shuddered and I let out a laugh. All I'd seen from Aimee's parents was sweet kisses, which really weren't anything bad.

Aimee spun in my arms and sliding her hands up my chest, she gripped my shirt, pulling me towards her. "If we have permission…then I guess…" Her lips pressed against mine in a sweet and gentle kiss. I wanted to deepen it but I knew we had to at least keep it PC since families surrounded us.

"I love you." The words fell out of my mouth as she pulled back and panic hit me, making my heart race. I didn't even know if she'd wanted the kids to be aware of how serious we were. The warm smile she gave me had me relaxing in an instant.

"I love you too," Aimee announced, before pressing another quick kiss to my lips. She patted me on the chest. "Now come on, let's go." She glanced at her watch. "We've got ten minutes to get to the big show. It'll be packed and we'll want good seats."

I stepped back, breaking my caged hold around her, and let her go.

Aimee walked a little in front of me and Dan slipped his hand into hers. She instantly looked down at him raptly as he told her something, his face animated and excited. She was an amazing, attentive mother and that in itself told me how they'd turned out to be such wonderful kids.

I spotted Matt and Sam in a sweet embrace a few meters away. "Put him down," I joked as I passed them, even though it warmed me to see them happy like that and I once again found myself grateful that they'd found each other.

I laughed when they jumped apart. "What? Did you forget you were in a public place?"

"No," Sam denied, but the frown on her face and the pink of her cheeks only confirmed my guess.

Matt wrapped an arm around her waist, pulling her into his side, and placed a quick kiss against her temple as we tried to catch up with Aimee, Sarah and the kids.

"So what animal are we heading to next?" Matt asked.

"Do you really care? I think you've spent more time watching Sam than any of the animals," I joked.

He playfully elbowed me in the side. "Like you can talk!"

It was true. I could barely take my eyes off Aimee on a normal day, and today she was wearing denim shorts that hugged her ass just right. I shrugged. "I'll take that."

———

THE DRIVE HOME had been quiet, the kids having dozed off early on into the thirty-minute journey. The odd outburst of *'jerk-face moron'*, coming from Aimee whenever someone cut her off, or just generally drove like an idiot in front of her, had my sides splitting with laughter and gave me the feeling that a road trip with Aimee behind the wheel would be even more entertaining than it had been with her as a passenger.

As Aimee reversed up the drive, the kids all woke up like there was some sort of alarm clock. It was kind of freaky.

I glanced at them over my shoulder. "You realize you guys are freaky, all waking up like that?"

The kids all shrugged like what I was saying was nothing new and I shook my head as they all filed out of the car. Turning my attention to Aimee, I watched her unclip her seatbelt, concern rolling over me when she didn't make a move to get out the car. "Are you okay?"

Taking a deep breath she nodded. "Yeah, just…ready for a nap."

I tucked a strand of hair behind her ear, letting my finger trail down her neck where I suddenly wanted my lips to follow. "A nap sounds good to me." I yawned. It was like the word had some magical power and I was immediately hit with a bout of tiredness I hadn't felt before then.

Sam pulled up beside us and, once her car rolled to a stop,

I opened my door and exited, walking around to meet Aimee at the other side.

My cellphone rang, and I pulled it out of my pocket, rolling my eyes as I saw Gary's name on the screen. I considered ignoring it, or telling him my cell wasn't connecting properly, but he'd have seen the photos from the zoo that I uploaded to Instagram and wouldn't believe me. And ignoring him wouldn't do me any good because he'd only try Matt next anyway.

I waved Aimee and the others in as I answered the call.

"Hello?" I never knew why, but I always answered questioningly, like I was uncertain who would be on the other end even when I'd seen the name on the screen.

"Saxton, you made it to the land down under." It was a statement, not a question, which confirmed that he'd been keeping tabs on my social media since I didn't actually tell him when I'd booked my flights. He would have probably wanted me to take security and no way in hell was I doing that.

God, Aimee's house was already full enough. Could you imagine adding a couple of security guys to the mix?

Matt and I had been extra careful with our posts, not stating where exactly we were or posting anything with identifiable sights, like advertising signs. We shouldn't have any problems with people following us around, it'd be too hard for them to find us in the first place. We could have been in any Australian zoo.

I sighed. "You know we did. What did you really call for, Gary?" Gary didn't call for no reason. There was always something he wanted, and I had a feeling I wasn't going to like whatever it was.

"I've been chatting with the label about your new sound."

"The sound you didn't like when we first came to you?" I knew I shouldn't have a dig, but it was pissing me off that he loved the sound now after he was dead set against it when we first went to him.

Gary carried on like I hadn't interrupted him. "We think you should add another guitarist to the band. In fact, we think you should add the guy from the gig you did."

I frowned. "Will? You think we should add Will to the group?"

"If that's his name…Yeah, Will…and your brother too. He's so much better than the keyboard player you currently have. The label will fly Will out to you guys in Australia and we expect you to come back in a month with a new song, or at least some ideas."

I couldn't believe what he was saying. "What? Why the hell does Will need to come out here? It's always been me who writes the lyrics with a little help on the melody from Matt." I stated, knowing he already knew this. I always made sure anyone involved in the songwriting process was credited. "Anyway, I don't even know if Will writes songs."

"We don't care if he writes. We want to make sure he has a good connection with everyone. What better way to do that than have you all together in Australia?"

I pulled the cellphone away from my ear and stared at the screen wishing I could see what the hell was going on in his head. "You do realize Kat and Alberto aren't here? They're back home spending time with my parents."

He hummed into down the line and I guessed he didn't. "I…just assumed… That's okay; I'll have them added to the itinerary and email you the details. Chat later, Sax."

"Wait!" I shouted as I was suddenly hit with a huge problem.

"Yes?"

"What are your plans for accommodation? Me and Matt are currently staying with Aimee and her family, and there is no way another three people will fit in the house."

"I'm sure you'll work something out," he stated before disconnecting the call.

I stared at the cell in disbelief before slipping it in my pocket and heading into the house, still shaking my head at Gary's plans. I found Aimee, Matt and Sam standing in the small entrance hall, obviously waiting for me.

Aimee's hand rubbed up my back, slipping beneath the t-shirt. The feel of her skin on mine sent shivers up my spine. "Everything okay?"

I shook my head. "I don't know. That was Gary. He's…" I rubbed a hand over my face not knowing what the hell to do about all this.

"Has someone found out where you are? Should we be expecting a stampede of paparazzi to turn up at the door?" Aimee asked, worry clear in her features as she glanced out the glass panels in the front door.

"It's nothing like that." I gave her a reassuring smile as she glanced back at me and her shoulders visibly relaxed.

"What did he want?" Matt asked, his brow furrowed in concern.

I sighed and had a feeling my own creased brow mirrored Matt's. "He wants to add Will and Al to the band."

"Will?" Matt questioned, his voice sounding an octave higher than normal. I wasn't surprised that he'd not mentioned Al, we'd all wanted him to join since we were signed but he had an aversion to the spotlight and we respected that. Unfortunately it looked like Gary and his team didn't.

"Yep, Will." I gave him a shrug and carried on. "He's booking a flight for Will, Al and Kat to come here for a month so we can mesh and write some songs."

"What about accommodation?" Matt asked, picking up on the same problem I had.

I forced out a laugh. "Apparently I'm going to work it

out." I gave him wide-eyes and a shrug, because fucked if I knew how I was going to work that shit out.

"Three extra people… We can make that work." Aimee stated, confident and sure. "There's a caravan with a double bed parked in the front yard so two people can sleep in there, and Dan can easily bunk with Chris and Reece, which will free up another bed."

Matt and I turned, shocked eyes on her. "Are you suggesting another three people move in here…for a month?"

She shrugged. "We'll have to run it past my parents, since it's their house and all, but I don't see why it won't work."

"Sounds like a good plan to me," Sam agreed nonchalantly as she headed through the French doors, towards the kitchen where Sarah was preparing dinner. "Do you need a hand Sarah?"

Sarah handed Sam a knife and pointed her in the direction of some veggies that needed cutting. "You two have had a long day on little sleep, Aims. Why don't you go for a nap?" Sarah suggested. "The kids are all occupied by their computers. We probably won't even see them surface again until dinner," she quickly added, as if she knew Aimee would bring them up.

Aimee's eyes fell on mine. "Does that sound good to you?"

I nodded, a broad smile crossing my face as I reached out and cupped Aimee's face. "Yeah, that sounds pretty perfect," I admitted before placing a gentle kiss on her lips.

"Thanks, Mum. If we aren't up in two hours, give us a nudge, please. Otherwise we'll be up all night again." Aimee called, grabbing my hand and pulling me towards the bedroom.

My dick twitched at the thought of going to bed even thought I knew that wasn't why we were going. I couldn't help but wonder if she'd be opposed to a quickie before drifting off to sleep.

I shut the door of the bedroom and turned, suddenly finding myself with my back pressed against the door. "I've wanted to do this all day," Aimee stated as she hooked her fingers in the waistband of my shorts and pulled them down as one with my boxers. My semi-hard dick sprang free and she dropped to her knees.

"Fuck!" I cursed as she engulfed my cock with her warm wet mouth, making it rock hard within seconds.

Aimee slid her mouth back up the length and let it pop free. "Ssh… we're meant to be napping," she reminded me and I pressed my fist to my mouth as she proceeded to torture me.

A sweet torture I never wanted to end.

CHAPTER TWENTY-FOUR

AIMEE

GARY HAD BEEN quick in organizing Al, Kat and Will's flight, and two days after the phone call Dom and I found ourselves standing on the other side of the arrivals doors waiting for two handsome guys—one all bad boy and tattooed, and the other sweet and innocent looking—and a beautiful rock chick to step through.

Will had been hesitant about joining the band at first, which was understandable. He did have a business to run after all. Thankfully another artist, along with Kelsey, was willing to help keep his shop going while he was gone. In the end Will had agreed to two weeks for the trip to test out if the five of them could meld together as a band. Only after that would he think about finding a more permanent manager for his store because that's what he'd need when they went back to touring.

Gary wasn't happy about the shorter duration, but he'd known it was that or nothing so he'd reluctantly booked the three of them return flights for two weeks later.

Their flight was an early six in the morning arrival time

and we'd been up since three thanks to the lovely jet lag that was still plaguing us.

I drank the last dregs of the double shot coffee we'd bought from the coffee stand when we'd arrived and groaned in disappointment.

"Let me guess, you've drank it dry and it didn't do a thing to wake you up?" Dom said, amusement clear in his tone.

I gave him a pouty sad face. "Yes. My coffee is gone and it's the end of the world." He pressed a kiss to the tip of my nose and I rose onto my tiptoes to place one on his lips.

"How come you two are always sucking face when I'm around?" The sound of Will's voice broke us apart and I turned to see him, Kat and Al coming to a stop before us.

"They're always sucking face," Matt stated, as both he and Sam had just come back from the coffee bar, their own cups in hand. "It's been a long time since we saw each other, Will. This is Sam."

I watched as they did the introductory handshakes and hugs.

Dom let go of my hand and gave him a manly hug. "And, fair warning, we don't suck face half as much as these two do." He hooked a thumb over his shoulder gesturing towards Matt and Sam.

I laughed at Sam's mock offended wide-eyes and jaw-dropped mouth. "You know it's true." I said as I gazed at her with a quirked brow.

Sam huffed, rolling her eyes. "Fine. Whatever." Her lips quirked and she couldn't repress her laugh any longer.

"Hey Aimee," Will surprised me by pulling me into a hug. "It's good to see you again."

"You too, Will." I relaxed into his embrace feeling genuinely happy to see him again. We'd had a good time on our night out and it was nice to think we had a chance at a friendship after all.

"Okay. That's enough. Get your hands off my girl," Dom stated gruffly, although his underlying laugh told us he wasn't serious.

Will released me from the hug but threw his arm over my shoulder instead. "No, I think I like having my hands on her."

I slapped at his side playfully. "Stop winding him up. Honestly, boys!" I slipped out from under his arm and headed for Al and Kat, giving them both welcoming hugs.

Dom had told me how close the five of them had been back in the day. They'd been the original band and he found it funny how they'd gone full circle to only come back together again now. Dom didn't seem to remember what had caused them to break apart—Will going his separate way—but whatever it was, it was nice to see them building bridges and having a second chance at their friendship. And band.

———

"Aims, the steak's ready, can you tell your mum to bring out the plates?" My dad called from his spot behind the barbecue. Behind the barbie had always been his place and he'd gotten good at cooking the perfect steak—along with his secret recipe burgers. He'd been making them since I was a kid and I was yet to find a better tasting burger.

I gave Dad a nod of acknowledgement and headed for the kitchen to let Mum know about the food and grab the plates or whatever else she'd want bringing out.

We'd decided a barbie to welcome the three newcomers would be nice for us all. There was nothing better than good food, drinks and a few board games to bring people together.

I placed the plates on the table telling everyone to take one and go get their steak from Dad. The rest of the food was in covered bowls and dishes on the table ready for everyone to help themselves.

The kids were the first to go up as usual. Teenagers seem to have a bottomless pit for a stomach.

It wasn't long before we were all seated around the large garden table, eating the food and enjoying the stories our five guests were sharing from their childhoods.

"Do you remember that time Dom was so fixated on his crush he walked right into a pole at school. *Boom!* And he hit the deck." Matt laughed.

"Oh god, yes. That was hilarious, it was on the way to assembly and the whole of our grade was making our way there." Will joined in laughing which seemed to be infectious because even those of us who weren't there all those years ago found ourselves chuckling along.

"How have I never heard this story before?" Kat asked before bursting into a fresh round of laughter.

Dom huffed. "I'm glad my teenage torment is entertaining you all."

I was sitting next to him so I squeezed his thigh under the table and leaned in to whisper in his ear. "Aww, babe. I'll make you forget all about it later." I placed a kiss on his cheek to cover my actions.

His thigh stiffened under my hand and I hazarded a guess that it wasn't the only thing hardening. He cleared his throat. "Sarah, have you got any stories about Aimee?"

My mum opened her mouth to speak but I jumped out of my seat and cut her off. "Oh look, everyone's finished. I guess it's time for desert."

Mum laughed and stood too. "I'll tell you all the embarrassing stories another time, Dom. There are plenty of them." She gave him a wink and I decided I'd have to make sure they'd never be left alone. I did not want Dom hearing all those things. Hell, I was still struggling to understand what Dom saw in the plain-Jane I was, I didn't need to add the stories of what a loser I was growing up into the mix.

As the hours passed the kids went to bed and my parents called it a night, so that they could go and watch their favorite show on Netflix, which left the seven of us chatting around the fire pit.

It was a nice warm night so the fire wasn't needed for heat, but the smoke kept the mosquitoes at bay and that was something you really needed—those bloodsuckers loved the humid Queensland nights.

Dom's fingers traced over the back of my hand, pulling my attention from Sam explaining the ins and outs of self-publishing.

I lifted my eyes to his and the far off look I saw in them had me concerned. "You alright?" I asked.

He shook his head as if he was shaking free his thought and put on a smile that I could tell was anything but real. "Yeah. I'm good."

I glanced from him to the others and made a decision to call it a night. Seeing Sam pause for a breath, I jumped in. "Hey guys, I'm heading to bed. Sam, can you make sure you smother the fire before you head in."

She nodded. "Yep, consider it done."

I stood and turned to Dom. "Are you coming with me or are you staying up to chat some more?"

Dom stretched in his seat. "I'm beat, I'll come too."

The guys laughed and some sexual innuendo flowed but I wasn't really paying attention, my mind was too busy thinking about how I'd get Dom to tell me about whatever was playing on his mind. I knew him well enough now to know there was something bothering him.

Dom led the way to the bedroom while I followed behind, quickly dashing into the boys' room to turn off Dan's dinosaur night-light as we passed. It ran on batteries and if I left it on the whole night I'd have to replace them the next day.

I entered the bedroom and closed the door behind me. Dom was at his side of the bed, his back to me as he pulled his shirt over his head and, without much thought, I walked over to him and ran my hands up his back sliding them around his waist before pressing a kiss to the center of his back. "Are you going to tell me what's on your mind?"

Dom turned in my hold, wrapping me in a warm embrace. I felt him press a kiss to the top of my head and smiled at how affectionate he was with me. My last relationship had lost any affection it had over the years, and it hadn't really had much to start with. What Dom gave me was a pleasant change.

I wanted to ask him again, but I figured he needed time to form the words or process whatever it was for himself. So I stayed there, wrapped in his arms with my ear against his chest listening to the rhythmic sound of his heart beating.

"It's been such a nice day. It just left me wanting…" The way he left his sentence hanging had me wondering if he was going to elaborate.

"Wanting?" I asked after a long few seconds of silence.

"I guess… I may be feeling how you felt before you knew I was coming to Australia with you. I'm loving being here, with you and your family, and the thought of me having to leave is niggling in the back of my mind."

I pressed a kiss over his heart and leaned back enough to look up at him. "I'm going to give you the same words a smart person gave me." I gave him a wink and his lips lifted at the corners. "I love you and I'm not letting you just walk out of my life. No matter what the future holds for us, we'll manage. If we have to do this long distance, we will. There will be many more family barbecues in our future."

Dom cupped my cheeks with his hands and pressed his mouth against mine. I opened to the swipe of his tongue and melted into him as he kissed me with everything he had.

I returned his kiss fervently. I wanted him to feel everything he was giving me because I loved this man with my whole heart and never wanted to have to live without him in my life.

CHAPTER TWENTY-FIVE

DOM - THREE WEEKS LATER

WE WERE all having such a good time that after just one week Will spoke to the guy looking after his studio, and asked if they'd be able to handle an extra week without him.

Obviously when Gary heard about the extra week he changed the dates for the three return flights, no questions asked.

Time had flown by and we'd all been getting along fantastically. In fact, it was like old times with the five of us jamming in the garage, only this time it had been Aimee's garage. We'd worked out a nice routine; Monday, Tuesday and Wednesday the five of us spent the days working on our music while Aimee and Sam wrote their books. The rest of the week we did all the touristy stuff or just hung with Aimee's family.

That all changed a few days ago when Matt altered his flight and flew out without any explanation. Afterwards we surmised that he and Sam had split, but Sam wasn't talking about it and Aimee was too worried about her to prod.

Will and Sam seemed to speak at length after Matt left — the three of them had been pretty inseparable since Will's arrival—and Will was soon calling Gary asking to change his own flight, which had me wondering what the fuck was going on.

Kat and Al flew home yesterday and when I spoke to Mom on my cell, letting her know they were on their way, she'd sounded so excited to be seeing them. I missed her and was glad it would be a while before we'd be ready to tour again.

I still had a few days left with my girl and planned to make the most of it.

I WAS in the kitchen making coffee for both Aimee and me when she ran out of the bedroom and bee-lined for the bathroom. She was so focused on reaching her target that she didn't manage to close the door, and I was soon hearing the sound of her vomiting.

Deserting the coffees as worry flooded my system I quickly strode to the bathroom. I found Aimee kneeling over the toilet bowl and gently reached out to pull her hair back. "That's it, let it out," I coxed as I stroked her back in big circular motions with my free hand.

After a few more retches Aimee wiped her mouth with a piece of toilet paper before dropping it in the bowl and sitting back.

"Better?" I asked.

She offered me a small nod of confirmation but the sight of her lips pressed together tightly told me she wasn't feeling very confident about it.

"I didn't realize you drank so much last night." I said, dropping her hair and thinking back to the previous night. She'd had a couple of vodkas while watching TV but nothing that should have given her a hangover. I'd seen her drink much more without suffering the next day.

"I didn't. It's not a hangover." Aimee turned her head to look at me but before her eyes reached mine she spun back around, a fresh bout of sickness hitting her.

Wiping her mouth once again, Aimee rested her forehead on her arm over edge of the toilet bowl.

"Can I get you anything?" I offered, feeling the need to help her as my hand kept on stroking her back.

"Ginger beer. Fridge in the garage," she said in a rush before leaning over the toilet once again.

Wanting to get Aimee what she needed and get back to her as soon as possible, I ran to the garage and quickly found a bottle in the door pocket. After pouring a glass, I left the bottle on the kitchen bench and went back to the bathroom to find Sarah sat on the edge of the bathtub stroking Aimee's back.

Aimee once again had her head resting on her arm and I held the glass out beside her. "Here," I offered. She gave me a brief smile as she reached for the glass before taking a tentative sip, followed by another.

"Aimee?" Sarah seemed to ask a whole question with just her name and Aimee nodded.

"I think so."

I glanced between the two of them trying to figure out what the hell was going on. Sarah's eyes caught mine and even though she could probably see the confusion written all over my face, she didn't explain anything. Instead she got up and left the room without a word.

Hearing the click of the door as it was closed I guessed Sarah didn't plan on coming back any time soon, so I decided to take her spot on the edge of the freestanding bath.

Aimee turned her head on her arm so she was facing me. Her hair was now roughly tied back. A loose strand across her forehead caught my attention and I tucked it back behind her ear.

"I think I'm pregnant," Aimee blurted out.

My mouth opened and closed of its own accord — I had no doubt I would've resembled a fish had I looked in a mirror — as Aimee's words pin-balled around my head not quite registering.

Aimee took another small sip of ginger beer and placed the glass on the tiled floor beside her, the clinking sound it made was loud in the small room. She reached out and gave my knee a gentle squeeze. "Are you going to say something?"

"I…Pregnant." I couldn't even form a sentence; my mind was feeling all hazy and the room tilted on its axis.

"Dom? You're as white as a sheet. You aren't going to faint on me, are you?"

A bright whiteness seemed to takeover my vision before my head was suddenly shoved between my knees and Aimee settled before me. "Breathe, Dom. In…and out… In…and out."

I followed her command and, slowly, the sight of my bare feet on the tiled floor became clearer as my mind became less muddled. "You think you're pregnant?"

"Yeah. I think so." There was something in her tone that I couldn't place so I lifted my eyes to hers. I was faced with a distant look in her eyes and a frown creasing her brow, which made me wonder what was at the root of that concern. "My periods are always irregular so I wasn't really worried about being a little late, but the sickness…"

I cupped her face in my hands and pressed a kiss to her scrunched up brow. "Don't stress. We'll figure it out." I pulled back grinning. "The sickness seems to have eased with my little…" I paused as I struggled to find a word for what had happened with me.

"Wobble?" Aimee suggested and I nodded. It was good

enough. "Well, I think it was the ginger beer that helped, but whatever it was I'll take it. I need to go find something to nibble on before it comes back."

My lips quirked. "I can think of *something* you could nibble on."

"Dominic Saxton! That *something* is what got us into this trouble in the first place." Her eyes twinkled with amusement and I couldn't help but beam back, my heart soaring with love for the woman in front of me.

Aimee stood and headed for the kitchen so I followed behind all the while wondering when we'd be able to find out for sure if she was pregnant.

Throwing away the two now cold coffees that had been all but forgotten, I made myself a fresh one as Aimee sipped on some more ginger beer while taking small bites of a plain cookie.

I took a long sip of the *elixir of life,* as Sam called it, just as the front door burst open.

Sarah walked in a white paper bag in her hand. She placed it on the breakfast bar where we sat and slid it in front of Aimee. "Go find out for sure."

Aimee looked at the bag and even I could see the terror in her eyes.

Abandoning my coffee I stepped up to Aimee, running a hand over her back. "Do you want me to come in there with you? I'm with you in this no matter what the result. Okay?"

Aimee took a deep breath and I could only assume it was to help calm her nerves. "Thanks, but I'm not sure I could pee with an audience." She quickly picked up the bag and slid off the stool she'd been perched on. "I'll be back in a minute."

Time seemed to stand still as I paced the small kitchen, waiting for the sound of the bathroom door opening again. I didn't even know what result I wanted her to come back with; I just wanted to know one way or the other.

"Dom, did you mean what you said…you'll be there for her?" Sarah's question caught my attention.

"Of course." I turned to face her, needing her to see the truth in my words. "One hundred percent." I hoped she heard the certainty in my voice because there was no way I would bail on Aimee if she were pregnant. I loved the woman with all my heart and I wanted her in my life for the long haul, baby or not.

Sarah nodded, seemingly satisfied with my answer, just as the bathroom door opened and Aimee stepped out, her face as white as the stick in her hand.

And in that moment, I knew my life was going to change forever.

The woman who owned me—heart and soul—was having my baby.

I was going to be a dad.

A mixture of terror and excitement filled me, and that alone was a little scary. But deep down I knew I didn't need to worry because there was one thing that I was certain of…

Aimee and I could get through anything, together.

CHAPTER TWENTY-SIX

AIMEE

KNOWING I'd be in for a long and sleepless night I stared at the ceiling in the dark room listening to Dom's soft snores as I worried about our situation.

After showing Dom the positive test, I'd booked a doctors appointment for first thing the next day, needing to get some official confirmation. I didn't expect a different result because by now I'd done another three at-home-tests that all produced the same positive result. I was certain that I was pregnant, still, I wanted to hear it from the doctor.

It wasn't like I didn't want more kids. Hell, with the way mine fought and argued on a daily basis, the way they answered back and were full of attitude at times, I felt like I'd failed them more times than not. But I loved them with all my heart and wouldn't want to live without them.

I'd love to have another.

To love another child unconditionally, and maybe with this child I wouldn't fail so badly.

But I'd had my kids at a young age and I knew what it was like to have to stop your life to raise kids.

I didn't want Dom to feel trapped.

I didn't want him to feel like he'd have to give up the career that he'd just started—a career he loved—to raise a kid with me.

If I thought I could do this alone and not fail again, I would…in a heartbeat. But that was where I went wrong before. My ex worked away and I was left to raise our kids alone. I couldn't do that to another child. I *wouldn't* do that to another child.

Dom rolled over and wrapping his arm around my waist he pulled me close. "I can almost hear your brain ticking," he mumbled groggily. I felt his lips brush over my cheek, a small puff of breath tickling against my skin. "Go to sleep," he added.

I turned on my side and snuggled into him so my back was against his front. "I'm sorry I disturbed you. I love you."

Dom's warm lips pressed against my back causing goose-bumps to breakout over my skin. "I love you too, sweetheart."

I closed my eyes, feeling in my heart that his words were the truth. It helped me relax knowing that no matter what was going to be happening in the future I was loved.

Loved deeply.

———

A SCREAMING match between Chris and Reece roused me from sleep. In fact, the whole house was woken by the loud argument. I leapt out of bed and charged through the house to referee.

Sibling fights had become a regular occurrence in our house, and their severity had amped up since the boys had hit teenage years. It was like the minute they become teenagers they received some kind of memo informing them that they should act like as big an asshole as possible and not to bother opening their mouth unless they were going to give one hundred percent attitude. It was no wonder I doubted my ability to raise another kid.

"*Oi!*" Grabbing a shoulder of each kid I tried to pull them apart and struggled because they were strong when anger was riding them. "That is enough. Get off him. Now!"

It was as if they'd suddenly registered I was there, as they both halted and turned their eyes on me.

"He started—"

"It was his—"

They both started blaming each other at once and I rubbed at my temples, feeling a headache coming on.

They went back and forth for a minute blaming each other and confusing me. If I was hearing correctly the argument had started because Chris thought Reece's earphones were too loud and they'd damage his ears. I shook my head; how did that turn into a wrestling match in the middle of the dining room?

I stared at them with wide eyes while they both complained about the other.

"Right. Okay… Chris, next time come to me and tell me that his earphones are too loud and I'll speak to him about it." He nodded and I turned my eyes on Reece. "Reece, if you feel Chris is being bossy with you, tell me instead of kicking off. Okay?" Reece huffed in annoyance but he also agreed with a reluctant nod.

I knew they wouldn't do what they'd just agreed to because they never did. They had the same stupid arguments over and over again, but at least I'd gotten them to stop for now and it had depleted the anger they'd been harboring.

As the adrenaline left my body, the fact that I'd moved without putting something in my stomach hit me as a bout of morning sickness washed over me.

Oh no!

Running for the bathroom I dived over the toilet just in

time, not surprised in the slightest that it was only bile that I brought up. Once my empty stomach was even emptier I wiped my mouth and took some deep breaths. I took a moment and assessed my body, trying to work out whether I should move to the kitchen to try and settle this with crackers and ginger beer, or if I needed to sit there a little longer.

"Aims?" Sam called out, knocking on the partially open door. "Are you okay?" I heard the door closing and shifting of material.

I turned my head to find her sat with her back against the door. "I'm pregnant."

There was no point in trying to keep it a secret. If this pregnancy was going to be anything like my previous ones, the sickness was only going to get worse and that would be a huge giveaway to someone who lived with you. There'd be no hiding it.

Sam's features seemed to fight with each other. Her mouth lifted into a smile, yet her brow moved into a frown, making it look like she was grimacing. "Why don't you sound excited about it?"

Feeling somewhat okay for the time being I shifted, settling my back against the bathtub opposite Sam. The bathroom wasn't huge and we could have easily touched toes if we wriggled our feet out a few more inches.

I sighed before I allowed my chaotic thoughts to tumble out of my mouth. "I love Dom more than I could ever imagine and having his baby…I don't have words to describe it." I rubbed at my chest as my heart started to ache. "But we don't know how our relationship is going to work. He's got to go back to America, record an album, and do a worldwide tour with Running Hearts. I don't know when I'll see him next. That on its own will put so much pressure on him, and to throw a baby into the mix?" I shook my head. "I don't want to be at the root of all that stress."

Sadness shone in Sam's eyes, but she didn't vocalize whatever she was thinking so I carried on.

"We're from completely different worlds. If we lived in the same country it would be so much easier, but I could never move there and he could never move here. Our lives are just too different, too far apart."

Sam nodded. "You're thinking about an abortion?" I wiped at a tear as it rolled down my cheek and for Sam that was answer enough. She shifted on the floor until she was beside me and pulled me into a hug. "Aims, you need to talk to Dom."

"I know." I wiped at an onslaught of tears as Sam held me together, being a friend I knew I didn't deserve. She'd gone through something herself over the last week, but she wouldn't speak about it, and I didn't know how to help her. Yet here she was helping me through my troubles.

A knock on the door stopped me from asking what was going on with her. "Aimee, are you okay? I've got a couple of crackers and some ginger beer for you." Dom's voice had my heart hammering in my chest.

I knew what Sam had said was right, but I had a feeling this was something Dom and I would never come to an agreement on. It was going to tear us apart and break both our hearts.

I wiped at my tears, grateful for the fact that I could pretend they were from the vomiting and nothing else. "I'm good. I'm coming out now."

Sam and I both got to our feet and I swilled my face with cold water in the sink before following Sam out of the door.

'Oh. Morning Sam. Do you want a coffee? I was just going to make one," Dom chatted away to Sam and I suddenly felt awful for putting her in this situation. I should have kept my thoughts to myself until I'd spoken to Dom about it.

I found the kids eating cereal at the dining table. Mum was sitting at the breakfast bar and Sam joined her while waiting on Dom to make their coffees. There was a glass of ginger beer on the side and a plate with some salted crackers on them, and I reached out to take one.

Dom turned at the sound of my cracker crunching. He pulled me into his arms and pressed a kiss to the top of my head. "Morning. How are you feeling?"

The coffee machine stopped making it's whirring noise and he released me to pass a cup to my mum before placing another for Sam under the spout and pressing the buttons on the top.

"I feel a little icky, but hopefully this will do the trick," I stated, holding the glass up before taking a quick sip.

The coffee machine finished again and Dom grabbed the cup. "Have you heard from Matt or Will?" Dom asked Sam as he handed her a steaming coffee.

Sam stared down at the cup in her hand like it was going to give her the answer to Dom's question. "No," she whispered before taking a sip of her drink and heading for the sliding door that lead to the back garden. "I'm going to drink this outside," she called over her shoulder to no one in particular.

"Fuck, I shouldn't have said anything," Dom said once she was out of earshot, his eyes following her movements through the kitchen window.

After finishing another cracker off the plate I walked over to Dom and ran a hand across his lower back and under his shirt. His skin warm and soft under my fingertips. "It's okay. I'll go talk to her."

Dom turned to face me, my hand sliding around his side and over the dips and valleys of his abs. "You're feeling better?"

"Yeah, my stomach is feeling settled, for now," I said as I

pulled my hand from under his shirt knowing I needed to head out to see Sam before the sickness came back. It was only a matter of time before the reprieve the crackers bought me would wear off. "I'll go find out what's happened, okay?"

"Thanks." Dom pressed a grateful kiss to my forehead and I hoped I could follow through on the promise I just made because if I got out there and Sam wouldn't talk, I couldn't force her to tell me.

Not knowing why his two closest friends left was weighing on Dom. Anyone could see it. And there was nothing I wanted more than to help him get answers, but they wouldn't come at the cost of my best friend's pain.

CHAPTER TWENTY-SEVEN

DOM

My eyes followed Aimee's movements, her hair glistening as the sun caught the golden strands. She sat down on a wicker chair across from Sam who didn't acknowledge her presence. They'd both stared off at the hills in the distance and I decided it was best for me to give them both the privacy they deserved.

Noticing Sarah had already vanished with her coffee, I grabbed my mug and headed for the bedroom thinking now was a good time to call home. Not only because, due to the time difference, I knew I'd manage to catch someone, but I was also desperate to talk to someone about everything that was going on. I needed to hear what my nearest and dearest thought of this.

Aimee had been distant with me since doing the first pregnancy test. I'd wanted to ask her what she was thinking, but I'd been so scared of what her answer might be that I didn't have the courage to utter the words.

Having kids wasn't something I'd really thought about, I'd never been in a relationship that serious. Yet as soon as Aimee had said that she could be pregnant, and the world had stopped tilting, I knew it was something I wanted. Hell, I was excited at the possibility, unfortunately my gut was telling me Aimee felt differently.

"Dom?" Mom's voice had me smiling even though it was underlined with worry.

"Hi Mom."

"What's wrong?" Mom asked, she sounded certain that all wasn't right.

I laughed nervously, not liking how well she seemed to read me. "Can't I just ring my mom without something being wrong?"

"You're not one to ring while you're away unless something's wrong, Dom. Tell me what it is."

I sat down on the bed and rubbed between my brows where I could feel a dull headache coming on. "Aimee's pregnant."

"Oh my gosh. Dom! That's…why do you sound so devastated?" Her confusion came through the line loud and clear and I could practically see her crinkled brow.

"I don't think she wants to keep it." Saying the words aloud had my heart hurting in my chest. It was like someone was squeezing it in a fist, making my breathing short. I forced myself to focus on taking some long, deep breaths, because I had a feeling I was having a panic attack.

"Have you asked her?"

I sighed. "I daren't."

"Dom, I know it's scary. Especially when you feel that she might not want the same thing you do, but you are meant to be flying back here at the end of the week. It's something you need to discuss before that happens." Mom was giving me her no nonsense voice and I knew every word she'd said was right, but it didn't mean I could follow through with the conversation I knew I had to have with Aimee.

"I know," I admitted.

The bedroom door opened and my eyes locked onto Aimee's as she walked in.

"Mom, I'm going to have to go. I love you and thank you."

"I love you too, son."

Aimee closed the door and paused with her back against it, watching me while I disconnected the call and placed my cell face down on the bedside table. I watched as she took a calming breath before speaking. "We need to talk."

I nodded. "You don't want to keep it, do you?" The words fell out of my mouth without thought. It was a question but I didn't need to hear her answer to know it.

A tear rolled down her cheek as she slid down the door and sat there with her back against it, her eyes closed. "I can't raise another child alone, Dom."

"I told you, I'm in this with you. One hundred percent."

Aimee shook her head. "You say that now, but your career has just kicked off, you have albums to write and record, tours to plan and play…Running Hearts are big now, and with this new sound you're gonna be massive. You can't do all that and raise a kid here at the same time." Anger was creeping into her voice and I couldn't decide whether it was aimed at her or me. "I can't up and move to America. Even if I wanted to I can't take the kids out of the state, let alone the country. My Douche-Fucking-Ex will make sure of that."

I knew what she was saying was true, but I just couldn't believe that we had no other options. Walking over I sat down beside her and took her hand in mine. "Surely we can figure something out. There has to be a way to make this work."

Aimee's cell chimed and she dropped my hand before standing and retrieving it from her desk. "I've got to get ready. I need to be at the doctors' in twenty minutes." The chiming stopped and I assumed it was an alarm she'd set to remind her about the appointment. I'd noticed she had a habit of setting alarms to remind herself to do things.

Aimee headed back towards me after grabbing some clothes. I wanted to stay there, rooted to the spot, and demand that we discussed it before she left the room so we could come to some kind of agreement but, sadly, I had a feeling this was one thing we'd never agree on. With a heavy heart, I stepped aside.

I reminded myself the doctor's appointment Aimee was getting ready for was just to confirm the pregnancy, which I was grateful for. At least that gave me more time to try to make her believe that we could raise this baby together without her fears coming true, because I was certain we could find a way.

We had to.

CHAPTER TWENTY-EIGHT

AIMEE

"AIMEE, PLEASE…" Dom reached out, brushing a strand of hair behind my ear, his eyes pleading.

It'd been three days since we had the pregnancy confirmed by the doctor. He'd given me a referral for an abortion clinic and had suggested I take a day or two to think it over. I made an appointment as soon as I got home.

Dom had spent two days coming up with ideas on how we could make it work but I knew none of them would work. He was willing to sacrifice too much, which meant he'd only end up resenting the baby and me.

"I'm sorry, Dom. I have to do this. I cannot deal with another child, not after everything."

He licked his lips, distracting me momentarily. "But this is *our* child."

Yeah, and I'd already had three others with my Douche-Fucking-Ex. I'd practically brought them up as a single parent because he worked away and look at how they turned out. I'd failed miserably. I'd tried to tell him that already time and time again over the last few days and all he'd say was that I was an amazing mum.

Dom was a rockstar. He'd have to travel and be away for long periods. I wasn't talking a couple of weeks at a time. I was talking months. I just couldn't live like that.

I couldn't fail another child.

A tear ran down my cheek and I turned my head, not wanting him to see the sadness in my eyes because I didn't want to have to see the hope in his. That would be instantly followed by heartbreak the moment he realized my sadness changed nothing.

A nurse called my name and I quickly wiped at my tears before giving her a nod to let her know I was coming.

I locked onto Dom's beautiful eyes and the heartbreak I saw in them almost tore me apart. "I'll understand if you're not here when I come out." I pressed my lips to his cheek and tasted salty tears, I didn't know if they were his or mine. "I'm sorry. I'm so fucking sorry," I said on a sob.

"Aimee…" he whispered my name as I walked away and my heart shattered in my chest knowing it was most likely the last time I'd ever hear my name on his lips.

Despite how many times Dom had said he was in one hundred percent, no matter what, I knew there'd be no us after what I was about to do. He'd never forgive me and, to be honest, I wouldn't blame him because I'd never forgive myself either.

The nurse gave me a sympathetic look as I sat down at the table before she slid a box of tissues in front of me. "Are you sure you want to do this?"

I nodded silently; because there was no way I could say it out loud. It would be a lie. I didn't *want* to do it, but it was for the best. I was a rubbish mother and I wasn't going to put another child through a life of having me as their only parent.

The nurse started talking me through the abortion process, explaining what would happen and when, almost repeating word for word what the doctor had told me only a few days earlier.

My mind trailed off and her words became background noise. Dom's heartbroken face was all I could picture. A face our baby could share.

Our child! Dom's words rang in my ears.

My stomach churned at the idea of destroying a life we'd created and I glanced around desperately looking for something to empty my stomach into.

Within seconds there was a medical sick bag in front of my face and I made good use of it.

Tying off the bag, I sat with my head between my knees taking in deep breaths, hoping to calm the nerves in my stomach.

My eyes met the nurse's as she offered her hand. "I'll get rid of that for you. There's another here if you need it," she said, placing a fresh one on the desk.

I let her take it, dropping my eyes back down to the charcoal grey carpet.

I can't do this. I. Can't. Do. This.

The words rang through my head and I knew it was true.

I couldn't kill Dom's child. My stomach finally stilled as I accepted that thought.

Desperate to explain my change of heart to Dom, I darted up, and quickly found myself on the floor, lightheaded from the sudden movement.

"Aimee," the nurse called out as she reentered the room, her worried eyes weighing me up.

I waved her off. "I'm okay. I just got up too quick." I tried to stand but she placed her hand on my shoulder and held me in place.

"No, stay there for a few more minutes while your blood pressure levels out again."

I shook my head. "No. I need to speak to the baby's dad. I

don't even know if he's still out there." I pushed myself up, ignoring the unhappy glare the nurse was giving me. I *needed* to find Dom.

I glanced around the waiting room, not surprised in the slightest when I didn't find Dom waiting for me. I'd known he wouldn't hang around. He was too heartbroken.

I kept going, heading for the car without pausing. He'd have to go back to the house even if it was just to pick his stuff up so that was my destination.

I made it home on autopilot. I barely remembered what junctions I'd stopped at and had no recollection of the traffic lights. I burst through the front door calling Dom's name.

"Dom! Dom!"

My mum came charging from her room. "What's happened Aimee? He looked devastated. He took all his stuff and left."

"How long ago?" I demanded, not wasting time answering her questions. If I weren't far behind, I had a chance at catching up with him.

"I don't know. Ten…fifteen minutes, tops." Mum sounded uncertain, but it was all I had to go on and, if she was right, there was a chance.

I turned, and charged out the door I hadn't even closed behind me. "Can you pick the kids up for me?" I called over my shoulder, knowing she would do so whether I'd asked or not.

"Yes. Drive carefully."

My neighbor waved as I pulled out the drive but I didn't wave back. I stared ahead, wondering whether I'd manage to find him before he disappeared out of my life. The only thing that gave me hope was the fact that his actual booked flight wasn't for another twenty-four hours. Although that didn't mean he wouldn't be able to get on another one once he'd made it to the airport.

Every car I sat behind, I wondered if he could be in it. When I passed them, he never was.

My hope started to dwindle with every minute that ticked by.

At the airport I pulled into the first empty space I found in the short stay car park and ran, following the departures signs. My eyes roamed the queues in the check-in area, my heart sinking when I didn't spot Dom.

I wanted to scream his name at the top of my lungs but all that would do was probably get me kicked out. Seeing a blonde woman dressed in the airline's uniform behind a counter without a queue, I ran straight for her.

"Hi! Can I help you?" She asked a broad smile in bright red lipstick on her face.

"I sure hope so. I'm looking for someone." I tapped my fingers nervously on the counter. "My partner and I had a misunderstanding. He wasn't due to fly until this time tomorrow, but I think he may have just changed his flight. I need to speak him. It's urgent. Is there any chance you can tell me which gate he'll be at or page him? Anything?" I forced myself to stop talking so she'd have a chance to say something.

She shook her head and a tear trailed down my cheek. "I'm sorry. I can't, it's against protocol."

"*Please!*" I begged. He needed to know I hadn't gone through with it.

"Can't you call him?" She asked, and I wanted to smack her for the stupid question.

"If I could do that, don't you think I would have? *Fuck!*" I couldn't contain my emotions; my voice had rose an octave or two.

I felt the security guard step up beside me before his deep voice reached my ears. "Miss, you need to calm down or I'll have to escort you off the premises."

I knew the woman wasn't going to help, so I turned my attention to the guy, hoping he'd feel bad for a damsel in distress. "My boyfriend is getting on a plane thinking I've had an abortion. I need to tell him I didn't do it." His eyes softened and I thought I might have won him over. "Please, if I give you his name can you go tell him?"

He weighed me up for a minute before glancing at the woman behind the counter. "Simone, give me his details and I'll go catch him before he boards."

Simone nodded and glanced at me her brow raised in question.

"Dominic Saxton."

She laughed a look of disbelief clear on her face. My straight look seemed to convince her a little because after a few seconds she typed his name into the computer in front of her. Her eyes widened and she scribbled something down on a piece of paper before passing it off to the security guard.

After a quick glance at the paper he pointed out a bench, telling me to take a seat until he returned, before dashing off at a pace I was grateful for.

I sat for a long twenty minutes waiting for the security guard to return. I never took my eyes off the door he'd gone through in case I missed him, and he'd forgotten what I looked like.

When he finally walked through the door, the disheartened look on his face told me everything.

I dropped my head into my hands as I wondered what the hell I could do to fix this mess I'd made.

"Miss, I'm so sorry but his flight had already boarded and the doors had been secured. I tried to get a message through via the crew, but I didn't have any luck." He sounded genuinely sorry as he reached out and patted my shoulder in comfort.

I wiped at the onslaught of tears that were running down my cheeks. "Thank you for trying."

"What are you going to do now?" he asked, clearly interested.

I shrugged. "I have no idea."

And that was the honest truth. Having been together twenty-four-seven we'd never felt the need to swap numbers. We hadn't even connected on social media because Dom hadn't wanted to risk my privacy.

When we'd been spotted out and about—which hadn't been often—I'd just been referred to as the mystery blonde. I think we'd been in two magazines in the whole month we'd been in Australia.

Dom had been right when he'd said the fans wouldn't believe the whole wife thing because that blew over pretty quickly, even after our kiss in the Honkytonk bar. People just don't have any trust in the papers anymore.

I don't know how long I sat there staring at the cracked tile under my feet, wondering how I was going to get a message to him. I'd have been able to get in touch through Matt if he and Sam were still on talking terms. Unfortunately, with their relationship having fallen apart, that was no longer an option.

My heart shattered at the possibility of never managing to get in touch with him, and I forced myself to take a deep breath before pushing away that thought.

I had to get in touch with him and that was that. I couldn't accept anything less.

I *wouldn't* accept anything else.

CHAPTER TWENTY-NINE

DOM

IGNORING my ringing cellphone for the sixth time in as many minutes I plucked at the guitar strings trying to find the right sound for the new song I'd been working on.

Two weeks had passed since I flew back home and I'd thrown myself into writing this album. It was the only thing that was getting me through the days. The only thing that occupied my mind enough so that I wasn't thinking about Aimee and the baby we'd never have.

"Dom?" Mom called through the closed door as she gently tapped on it. "If you don't come down and eat something…I'll be forced to join you in your hunger strike."

I rolled my eyes. Out of all the things she could have threatened me with, she had to choose the one that would work. I sighed as I placed the guitar on the bed. "Okay."

I pulled open the door and was surprised to see how shocked my mom looked.

"Okay? You're actually coming down?"

The feeling of my lips quirking in the corners at her surprise felt foreign and they soon dropped back into the grimace I'd been sporting for the last couple of weeks. "Yes, Mom. I'll come down to eat."

The smile that graced her face made me realize I was doing the right thing. I'd clearly been worrying her over the last few days and I suddenly felt ashamed about that. She wrapped her arms around me in a hug and I willingly hugged her back. "You should probably shower before you make your way down too," she stated as she stepped back, her face screwed up in a grimace like she smelled something bad.

I was about to argue that I didn't smell that bad but realized it would have been a lie. I couldn't even remember the last time I'd showered. I ran a hand over my jaw as I contemplated a shower and felt a good week's worth of scruff there. *Could it really have been that long?*

I hung my head in the shower as the warm water beat down on my neck and back. Thoughts of Aimee ran through my mind and I didn't try to push them away, I needed to face it even if it was only for the five minutes I was in the shower. I wondered what she was doing.

Was her heart be hurting as much as mine?

I didn't even need to think about that. I knew it would. It wasn't an easy decision for her and I understood her reasoning. That's why it hurt so much. I couldn't exactly argue with her so I had no way to change her mind. As much as I wanted to support her, I couldn't have stuck around for her. I had to leave even if that meant I was leaving my heart and soul with her. There was no other way.

I'd broken my resolve once or twice and checked her Instagram account—it wasn't hard to find her online since her accounts were all public due to her writing—hoping to see something from her, but from the look of things she hadn't posted anything new since I'd left.

As I stepped out the shower I wrapped a towel around my waist and headed back for my room to find some clothes and get dressed. My cell rang yet again and this time I picked it up. Not recognizing the number I answered cautiously.

"Hello?"

"Saxton? My name is Rachel. I work for TMZ. Is it true that your mystery blonde in Australia had an abortion?"

My heart leapt into my chest. *How the fuck did they know about that?*

My name had never been on any of Aimee's medical records in regards to that. *Had Aimee sold her story to the papers?*

I couldn't ask them how they knew without giving them their answer. Thinking quickly I asked the only thing I could. "How did you get this number?"

"That doesn't matter. If you'd like to make a statement before the story gets published…" she pushed on, leaving the sentence hanging in the end.

"The fact that the only people who have this number are trusted means someone has betrayed me by giving a scumbag like you my number. So yes, it does matter." I countered.

She must have realized I wasn't going to confirm or deny the story, because she quickly disconnected the call and I stared at the screen wondering whether to Google my name and abortion to see what I could find. The thought that it could be Aimee stopped me from doing it. I didn't know what I would've done if she'd sold a story about us. *Our story.* I couldn't live knowing she wasn't who I'd thought she was.

"Dom. Your food's getting cold," Mom called up the stairs and I threw my cell on the bed before temptation got the best of me. A temptation that I knew would nag at me until I gave into it, but I was determined to ignore it for as long as I could.

My heart was hurting enough as it was, I didn't need more to add to that pain.

CHAPTER THIRTY

AIMEE

THE SAND beneath my feet was cool as I strolled along the beach. The cold bite of the winter's breeze blew my hair in my face and I couldn't help but wish I'd tied it back. Feeling my wrist with my fingers, I noticed I didn't even have my usual spare hairband on there and decided pulling it back and knotting it around itself was as good as it was going to get.

Finding a clear spot on the deserted beach, I sat down and stared out at the waves. Watching the ocean had always been calming and, as my hand dropped to the small bump under my top, I felt myself relaxing with the ebb and flow of the water.

I'd spent the first six months of this pregnancy writing emails and messages to anyone that I thought could get me in contact with Dom. Unfortunately, I hadn't had any luck.

Knowing Dom ran his own Instagram account I'd even tried sending him messages, but I never received any replies and I told myself it was just that they were getting lost in the sea of messages he must get on a daily basis. I couldn't handle the thought that he was ignoring me intentionally.

Lifting my phone I stared at the number of my last resort —Gary, Dom's record manager—wondering whether this might be the sliver of hope I'd thought it was when I'd found his number. Aware that there was only one way to find out I bit the bullet and pressed call before I could come up with an excuse to chicken out.

My heart hammered in my chest when he answered after just one ring.

"Gary Michaels, Blackwall Records, what can I do for you?"

I swallowed the lump in my throat before taking a calming breath. "Hi. My name is Aimee. I met you a few months ago with Dominic Saxton. You know, the whole wife thing." I knew I was babbling but I couldn't seem to stop myself.

"Ah, yes. I remember, although that doesn't tell me why you're calling."

I had no idea what I'd been thinking ringing Gary. What the hell was I meant to say? "Well, I was hoping you could get me in touch with Dom. We had a misunderstanding before he left and I need to clear it up."

He made a noncommittal tutting noise on the other end of the call and my hopes fell. "I'm sorry, I can't release information like that."

"Look Mr. Michaels, can't you just give him my number?" Deciding hitting him with the cold hard truth was probably my best option, I let the words fall out of my mouth. "Dom thinks I aborted his child. I need to tell him I didn't. I need to tell him he's going to be a father."

"I'm not going to pretend I know what happened between you two, but he's written his best stuff since he came back from Australia. This kind of news could change the direction of the band's music completely, and I'm not willing to take that risk by passing on your news. I can do one thing for you, and that is give you money so you and your child will want for nothing. That's all I can offer you."

I scoffed. "I don't want your money, or Dom's for that matter. I love him and he deserves to know he has a child in the world. Those songs you talk about are full of pain and heartache. I want to help him heal the wounds he shouldn't even have."

"Well, then I'm sorry Aimee, but there's nothing I can do to help you."

I didn't wait to hear if he was going to try and explain himself more. I disconnected the call and dropped my phone back into my bag before wiping away the angry tears that were rolling down my cheeks.

I couldn't understand how someone could be such a self-centered asshole. I knew it was business to him, but this was Dom's life we were talking about. His wellbeing even.

I'd heard a couple of Running Hearts's new songs, the ones Gary had been talking about, and he was right. They were good—*really* good—but they were also heartbreaking, filled with pain and loss. I didn't even listen to the radio anymore because I couldn't bear to hear them when they came on, and trust me when I tell you they came on all the time.

I rubbed my hand over my bump as I felt a foot move across my stomach. "I guess we'll have to wait until you're here before we go and find your Daddy," I said, having gotten used to talking to the bump over the last few months.

I hadn't wanted to worry my parents over my stress. They were already worried about me, considering how badly the morning sickness was still affecting me.

The morning sickness was the only thing that was keeping me from jumping on a plane to New York and attempting to find Dom's parents' house or camping out at Gary's office until Dom turned up. I wasn't the best of travellers normally and this pregnancy was kicking my ass. I could barely keep a meal down and I'd been admitted to hospital and put on an IV for fluids more than once in the last six months. I knew there was no chance of me managing a flight.

"Hey, I thought I'd find you here." Sam's voice pulled me away from my thoughts and I turned to watch her as she sat beside me.

"You thought right," I said, giving her a smile. "How are you doing?"

Sam had been quiet and somber since things fell apart with Matt. She didn't talk about it, even when I tried my hardest to get any information I could out of her; she kept it all close to her heart. She had secrets and I felt a little sad that she didn't feel she could share them with me — after all I was meant to be her best friend and that was what besties were for — but I respected her wishes and tried not to take it to heart, knowing if she really needed to talk it out she would come to me.

She shrugged. "You know…same old shit, different day."

I glanced back out at the sea. "Yeah, I know the feeling." Reaching out I grabbed her hand, which had been resting on her knee and wrapped my fingers around it, giving it a squeeze. "I'm here for you. Always. You're my sister by choice and I'll do anything for you."

Pulling her hand back, she wrapped her arm around my shoulders giving me a side hug and pressing our heads together. "Right back at you, sweetie."

We both stared out at the ocean, lost in our own thoughts until Sam broke the silence. "So, what's the plan? How are we going to get you your man?"

Sam was the least optimistic person I knew so I couldn't help but laugh at her sudden optimism. "I guess we wait until bump arrives and we take a flight to the first event I can find that he's attending."

"Go complete stalker... I like it!" The grin on Sam's face was a welcome sight. I hadn't seen her genuinely happy for months and it made me beam in return.

Maybe there will be a light at the end of the tunnel after all.

CHAPTER THIRTY-ONE

DOM

MY FACE ACHED with the fake smile I'd had plastered on for the last hour. As much as I wanted to drop it, being nominated for a Country Music Award was a massive thing and I had to at least look happy about it.

It wasn't like I didn't appreciate the nomination, but the song that had been nominated was my most painful one. Full of memories I'd just wanted to forget. I guessed that was the downfall of being a songwriter. By the time you were ready to try to come to terms with whatever had inspired you to write the song in the first place, the song was popular and you found yourself having to sing it time and time again, reopening that wound you were trying so desperately to heal.

In saying that, I knew this wound would never heal completely. I'd lost two of the most precious people in my life and one of them had never had a chance to live.

The pretty blonde model hanging off my arm drew my attention as she tugged on my elbow. "Saxton, they want photos." She pointed down the red carpet towards another group of paparazzi that'd just finished shooting Kat and her plus one, a new artist Gary was trying to drop into the spotlight. There had been talk of him being the opening act for our next tour but we hadn't had a chance to listen over his work to decide if we thought he'd fit.

The photographer was waving Matt, Will and Al over too so they clearly wanted a full band shot. No one else had bothered trying for one so I was impressed, but not enough to be happy about having yet another photo taken.

We'd been posing for the last twenty minutes and, quite frankly, I was sick of it. Still, I allowed the model, Mariana, to pull me along and didn't let my fake smile drop.

I'd been a bit of a recluse since getting back from Australia and Gary thought it would be good for my image if I were seen at my first event with a pretty lady on my arm. I couldn't care less about my image but, if it got him off my back, I was willing to do it.

Mariana didn't expect anything to happen between us and that was all that mattered to me, because I wasn't looking for any kind of relationship.

I sighed and leant in to whisper in her ear knowing the cameras would love the intimate shot. "Please tell me we can go get a drink soon."

Mariana threw her head back in a laugh, clearly faking it because I hadn't said anything that funny. "Well, we can go in but sadly you can't drink until you've performed."

I groaned as I straightened. "Why did I agree to that?" Only part of me was joking. The song was going to rip me apart and sour my mood completely. I wasn't certain I could handle that.

The Running Hearts members all stood together looking happy for the cameras when none of us really were. We all seemed to have our own issues lately, ones that we didn't care to share with one another.

As we walked past a crowd of fans along the edge of the red carpet, people started calling out my name and Mariana let go of my arm. "Go, Saxton," she said with a smile and I felt my own become less forced.

One thing that actually made me happy these days was interacting with fans, seeing how much they appreciated getting a selfie with me or just having me scribble on a piece of paper for them. My autograph was illegible and changed from one to the next but with every one that I did, the recipient seemed to look at that scrap of paper like it was a priceless treasure.

"Saxton," a young brunette called and I smiled at her and her friend. "Can we have a selfie?" She held out her cellphone and I took it, turning so that the three of us were in the shot before handing it back to her. She held her cellphone to her chest as she thanked me.

Another person called my name and I gave them my attention next. Followed by another and another.

After about fifteen minutes of signing things, smiling for selfies and shaking hands, a bell sounded through the air and a newfound energy ran through the crowd. It was the ten-minute warning. We all needed to get inside and find our seats before the cameras started rolling and the show started. Mind you, the cameras were already rolling, people loved watching the stars arrive and walk the red carpet.

Mariana stepped up to my side and, just as I'd started to stride towards the door, someone called my name. My *real* name.

"Dom!"

I didn't need to turn around to know who it was. It was a voice I'd never be able to forget. I closed my eyes and could see her beautiful green eyes as clear as day. My heart stuttered in my chest at the knowledge that the woman who owned my soul was within reach. Aimee was somewhere in that crowd.

"Saxton." Her voice sounded uncertain and that alone had me turning on the spot.

I *needed* to see her.

I needed to know I hadn't imagined her voice, when really it was just a fan.

I didn't have to search the crowd for her, my eyes instantly landed on the gorgeous figure that stood at the front of the crowd. The uncertainty I'd heard in her voice was clear on her face, she had a worried frown that I just wanted to kiss away.

Not even conscious of moving, I suddenly found myself standing inches before her just the rope hanging between us, even though it felt like a great big crater.

My eyes flitted around her face, taking in the underlying sadness I could see there and the dark circles around her pain-filled eyes. She looked as bad as I imagined I did and it didn't make me feel any better about the situation. As much as over the months I'd wished I wasn't the only one suffering, seeing her angst now had me wishing I could take it all away from her.

There was a noise and Aimee shifted. I caught sight of her hand patting at her front and I dropped my eyes to a bundled up baby tied to her chest in what looked like a sling.

My heart leapt into my throat and I opened my mouth to speak when her other hand came into view and she held out a piece of paper and pen. I frowned at her and she shook her head, her eyes imploring me to just go with it.

Reaching out I took the paper, feeling a folded-up piece underneath it. I discreetly slipped it into my pocket and scribbled an autograph on the other before handing it back with the pen.

"Thank you," is all she said as she stepped back into the crowd while she shushed the now wailing baby.

Our baby.

Dazed and confused, I was led into the venue. I couldn't seem to focus on anything and the only thing I recognized was the gold material of Mariana's dress that was trailing by my side. We came to a stop and she pressed a hand on my shoulder in an effort to make me sit. I dropped into a chair, mildly grateful that there was actually one beneath me.

A glass was pressed into my hand and I stared at the golden liquid inside it.

"Drink. I don't know who that was or what it meant, but it shook you up and you need a drink," Mariana's words pulled me out of my daze and I rooted in my pocket for the piece of paper Aimee had handed me.

Standing in a panic, I discarded the glass on the table not caring as the liquid sloshed over the edge and soaked into the tablecloth. I dug deep into both my pockets, not remembering which one I'd put it in.

Relief flooded my body as my fingertips brushed against the sharp edge of a folded piece of paper.

I closed my eyes and paused as I took a deep calming breath. My chest ached with the air it received, making me think that I hadn't breathed properly since I'd heard Aimee's voice.

"You okay, Dom?" Matt asked and I glanced at the table to see my family and band mates all watching me, concern clear on their faces.

"I…" I didn't really know the answer to that, not until I'd read the note at least. I pulled the small piece of paper out of my pocket and unfolded it with shaky hands. Mariana wrapped her hand around mine, holding it steady enough for me to be able to read the words on the paper.

Hilton Garden Inn - Room 105

I wanted to bolt out of there right then and there, but I knew I couldn't. We had to perform and, if I was lucky, we had an award to accept.

"Dom?" Mom's shaky voice sounded beside me and I looked across at her as she read the words on the paper. "What's going on?"

A tear rolled down my cheek as I pulled my mom into a hug while tucking the piece of paper back into my pocket. I wanted to keep that slip of paper forever. I wanted to frame it.

"Everything has fallen into place, Mom." My smile made my cheeks hurt and I wanted to explain everything, but I didn't know enough to able to. If I told them anything, they'd have more questions than I had answers, so I decided to just leave it as that. I could tell them more once I'd seen Aimee and that was something I was going to do as soon as the awards show was over.

There was no chance in hell I'd be going to the after party.

No, I had a note burning a hole in my pocket and a hotel room to get to. I was going there at the earliest possible convenience.

———

I STARED at the shiny silver numbers on the solid wooden door before me as I stood with my arm poised, ready to knock. It was one-thirty in the morning and I started to doubt whether coming at this time had been a good idea. There was a baby in there and my knocking could wake it up. What if Aimee had expected me to come in the morning sometime?

Knowing I wouldn't be able to sleep until I'd spoken to her, I hoped she felt the same and quickly rapped my fist against the door, trying to be as soft as possible to not the wake the baby, yet still loud enough to be heard.

There was a click on the other side of the door and I assumed Aimee had released the security latch that some hotel doors have. Her pretty, make-up free face appeared in the gap as she opened the door, a broad smile gracing it when she saw me. The sight took my breath away.

"I didn't know if you'd come," Aimee stated as she stepped back opening the door wide in invitation.

I stepped in, pausing as I waited for her to close the door. I glanced around the room not able to really see much in the semi darkness. The only light was coming from a dim lamp beside the bed and it looked to have something laying over it to make it even duller. All was quiet, and I assumed the baby must've been sleeping.

"I hoped you'd come, but…I wouldn't have blamed you if you didn't." Aimee's voice sounded timid, something I hadn't heard from her before and I didn't like it.

Turning to face her I reached out with a finger, placing it under her chin and lifted until her eyes connected with mine. "Aims, you came all this way. I had to."

Her sage green eyes welled with tears and she blinked. "I'm sorry," she claimed, quickly dashing away the escaped tears with her fingers. "I've missed you."

Aimee's admission had me wrapping her in a warm embrace. "I've missed you too." In that moment I didn't care what had or hadn't happened all those months ago. All I cared about was that I had the woman I loved in my arms where she belonged.

A baby's cry came from the direction of the bed, causing Aimee to pull back out of my hold and I let her go.

"I guess someone wants to meet her daddy."

"Her?" I asked with wide eyes.

Aimee nodded before walking around the bed and leaning into a bassinet I hadn't noticed before. She flicked at some switches on the wall beside the bed and a couple of the lamps scattered around lit up, bathing the room in a warm glow.

I couldn't move as she walked towards me. It was like my feet were cemented in place.

She grinned down at the baby in her arms. "Hey beautiful, are you ready to meet your daddy?" The baby's wails quieted down, as if she'd understood the words, when in reality she'd probably just recognized her mom's voice. Aimee came to a stop before me, meeting my eyes as she placed the baby in my arms. "Meet Thea-Rose Saxton, your daughter."

Thea-Rose had a head full of dark hair, reminding me of baby pictures I'd seen of myself, and I couldn't help but grin. Feeling the need to sit, I stepped over to the bed and perched on the edge, not taking my eyes off Thea's baby blue orbs looking back at me. She was beautiful. Absolutely precious.

I felt a tear run down my cheek before a gentle finger wiped it away. I glanced up to find Aimee standing beside me, tears running down her own cheeks. I shifted Thea in my arms until I had a spare one and patted the bed beside me. Once Aimee joined me I placed my arm around her shoulders, pulling her into my side.

Laying her head against my chest, Aimee watched Thea and, in that moment, I knew my life was exactly how it should've been.

My heart bursting with love for the two beautiful girls in my arms...

Right where they belonged.

EPILOGUE

AIMEE - TWO YEARS LATER

DOM'S light feathery kisses worked their way up over my enormous bump as he followed the baby's kicking foot, causing goosebumps to break out over my skin. Not to mention the pulsating down below that was making me squeeze my legs together. "Dom…I…"

"Again?" He lifted his head and locked his gaze on mine, his raised eyebrows telling me how shocked he was, if his high voice wasn't already any indication.

This pregnancy had sent my sex drive into a crazy level of horny. I'd always heard pregnancy could affect women that way, but my previous pregnancies had only been affected mildly.

This one?

This one was amped up to the max. All Dom had to do was glance in my direction from across the room and I was desperate for his touch.

"You'd best make the most of it, because once the baby comes I might never want sex again," I teased, knowing he'd give me what I needed regardless of the threat, because that was what Dom did. He always gave me everything I needed, as I did him. That was how a good relationship worked.

The one thing Dom couldn't give me was him living here permanently. I knew what it was like to live away from your family and that was something I'd never ask of him.

So Dom traveled a lot. Thankfully, he'd managed to spend most of the pregnancy here, which had been wonderful because he'd missed out on it all when I carried Thea. Seeing his face full of wonder as he stared at the screen during each and every ultrasound brought tears to my eyes.

I'd felt ridiculously guilty for him not experiencing that before, even though I'd done everything I could to get touch with him—even ringing his record manager, Gary. It was something that I felt would forever haunt me.

After Dom had found out about Gary's actions he'd refused to work with him any longer and the band whole-heartedly agreed. Luckily, they'd managed to get out of their contract without any consequences and another record company snapped them up. It had been a bit of a blessing in disguise because the new company allowed them to record in both Australia and America—which gave Dom the chance to be here more often than not—and they'd given them a bigger, better budget for their tours.

"Well, in that case…" Dom's hanging sentence pulled me back to the moment and I caught sight of his mischievous smirk before he moved lower with his feathery kisses.

I felt his warm mouth through my knickers and squirmed on the bed. I needed the barrier gone and I needed his mouth on *me*. I moaned as he ran his tongue over the edge of the material, sending shivers of anticipation through me.

Dom's fingers hooked in the waistband and he made quick work of tugging them down my legs before I felt his hot breath against my core.

I bit at my lip as I tried to watch him, only to be impeded

by my bulging stomach. My hands fisted the sheets at my sides when his tongue flicked out to run up the length of my lips before it swirled around my clit. I raised my hips needing more and, knowing exactly what I needed, his finger slipped inside.

"Dom!" I cried out as he worked his magic bringing me to the edge of orgasm in no time.

"Let go, Aims."

My body instantly followed his command and I came, my core clenching around his fingers.

"That's it Baby," he praised as he removed his fingers, sending a fresh set of shockwaves through me.

Dom pressed kiss after kiss up my body before he lying beside me. I wanted to turn to him but I was still coming down from my orgasm and couldn't quite bring myself to move just yet.

When I felt like I at last had control over my body once again, I opened my eyes and spotted a small gift-wrapped box sitting on top of my bump. It was wrapped in green paper with red candy canes, a gold ribbon tied around it in a bow. I flicked my eyes to Dom questioningly.

"I know we'd said we'd wait for everyone to arrive before exchanging gifts but I wanted to give you this one when it was just us," he explained, worry written all over his face.

I struggled to sit up and the little package fell off my bump.

Dom shifted and helped me to sit up with my back against the headboard before passing me the present. "Merry Christmas, Baby." He pressed a quick kiss to my temple and I leant into it, loving his affectionate ways.

The present was so nicely wrapped, I felt bad destroying it all as I pulled the bow loose. Once the paper was gone, I was left holding a purple box. I gave Dom a curious glance before flicking the lid open.

I gasped as my eyes roamed over the beautiful ring inside.

"Aimee, I love you more than anything in the world, and I think it's about time I listened to Beyoncé and put a ring on it. Will you marry me?" Dom's eyes were pleading and I felt mine fill with tears.

"Yes…Yes." My hands shook and he steadied them, wrapping his hands around mine. "I'll marry you." I crushed my lips against his in a messy kiss full of love.

Breaking the kiss, Dom leant back and pulled the ring out of the box. "Let's put this where it belongs then." He slid the white gold ring on my finger and I stared at the square diamond as it glistened in the light coming through the open blinds at window. It was beautiful.

Living through a Queensland summer was like living in the pits of hell. The humidity was beyond ridiculous and you had no choice but to leave the windows and doors open all night in the hopes of getting a slight breeze to help you sleep, if only for a couple of hours. You got to be woken up by the twittering birds and the rising sun. Some people would call that beautiful, but I'd always loved my sleep and often referred to it as a pain in the ass.

"Perfect!" Dom stated as we both admired the ring, which fitted my finger just right.

I cupped his face with my hands and pressed another kiss to his lips. "I love you," I declared, leaning back just enough to get the words out before going back in for another kiss.

Dom ran his tongue along the seam of my lips and I opened up welcoming him in. I'd never get enough of his kisses and now I was going to get to enjoy them for the rest of my life. I couldn't help but wonder how I'd been so lucky to be able to call this wonderful man *mine*.

The sounds of Thea chattering to herself crackled through the baby monitor on the bedside table. I pulled back and rested my forehead against Dom's as I took a moment to regain my breath.

Dom's heavy breathing told me I wasn't the only one affected and the thought had me grinning.

"I best go get her before she starts shouting the house down and wakes everyone else," I suggested as I made a move to get up.

Dom nudged me back on my pillow. "You relax. I'll get her, she can help me make pancakes."

I glanced at the clock and seeing it was only six in the morning I knew I had no time for more sleep, I needed to get up and prepare the turkey so it would be cooked in time for when we wanted to sit and eat. I had a houseful of guests that needed a good Christmas dinner.

Last Christmas, we'd travelled to America and spent the holiday period with Dom's family and friends. We'd been thrilled when they had agreed to travel to Australia for this one. If I'd known I would be heavily pregnant, I would've probably preferred a quiet one instead. Although just seeing all our loved ones, smiling and happy in one place, made up for having to cook a full Christmas dinner in ninety percent humidity and thirty-plus degrees Celsius temperatures.

I gave Dom one last peck before letting him go and flashed him a grateful smile. "Thank you. I'll be out soon, I've got veggies and turkey to prep."

He gave me a knowing smile. "The house is brimming with people, I'm sure you're going to have plenty of helping hands." He frowned. "Actually, you might have too many."

I laughed. He was definitely right about that. They didn't say *'too many cooks spoil the broth'* for nothing.

I was certain I'd be falling over people all day, but I wouldn't want it any other way.

Family was everything to me, and always would be.

A sparkle caught my eye and I couldn't help but admire

the ring on my finger once again. It caused a thought to suddenly hit me…

Dom and I were getting married.

Our families were officially becoming one big one.

In the beginning I'd been certain that Dom would own my heart and soul, but I never would have guessed he'd have my hand too.

ACKNOWLEDGMENTS

There are so many people who support me on a daily basis and I love them all dearly for it.

First and foremost, *my family*. Thank you for keeping me grounded and not letting me lose myself in these characters and their worlds.

Kamisa Cole, you girl, go above and beyond to push me out of my comfort zone. You'll never know how much you inspire me. This story wouldn't exist if it wasn't for you. Thank you for always believing in me. I love you tons.

To my editor, *Jane*, thank you for polishing this up to the pretty package it is now. I look forward to working with you on the next one.

Marisa, you really are a cover designing goddess. I love your work.

To anyone reading this, thank you for picking this book up and giving it a chance. You are incredible!

ALSO BY SAFFRON BLU

Running Hearts Series

Running Hurt - *Dom & Aimee*

Running Scared - *Matt* (Coming late 2019)

Running Wild - *Kat* (Coming early 2020)

Running Free - *Al* (Coming late 2020)

Anthologies

Love is Love - Break Away

www.ingramcontent.com/pod-product-compliance
Lightning Source LLC
Chambersburg PA
CBHW071524110726
47908CB00003B/938